I BACKED ... PUSHING ... ...ARDS THE FRONT DOOR. "GO OUTSIDE," I SAID SOFTLY.

She tried to move around me, to see what I'd seen. I turned and grabbed her by the shoulders. "Get outside and use my radio to call in. Tell 'em who you are and where you are, and tell 'em to send a squad car immediately."

"Rebecca!" Melissa said, trying to get around me again.

I shoved her out the door. "Do what I say!" I shouted, watching for a second to make sure that she would.

I backtracked into the foyer and went straight ahead to the kitchen. The place was a mess. And written in something red, something I hoped to hell was ketchup, on the wall next to the door to the utility room, were the words, "nigger-lover."

───────── ★ ─────────

CHASING AWAY THE DEVIL

SUSAN ROGERS COOPER

WORLDWIDE.

TORONTO • NEW YORK • LONDON
AMSTERDAM • PARIS • SYDNEY • HAMBURG
STOCKHOLM • ATHENS • TOKYO • MILAN
MADRID • WARSAW • BUDAPEST • AUCKLAND

CHASING AWAY THE DEVIL

A Worldwide Mystery/October 1993

First published by St. Martin's Press, Incorporated.

ISBN 0-373-26129-2

Printed in U.S.A.

To Don and Evin, always, and to
my big brother, Frank Rogers,
for his support, honesty,
and enthusiastic response

ONE

THE THIRD WEEK of November is Pioneer Week in my home, Prophesy County, Oklahoma. There's nothing in this goddamn world I hate more than Pioneer Week. They make us deputies dress up for it. In chaps. And cowboy hats. And boots. And spurs. And real-live six-guns on our hips. It's goddamn ridiculous.

I had more important things to do than dress like an idiot. Less than a month before, I lost my garage and some other stuff to a tornado. And now I had contractors all over the goddamn place with only my sister Jewel to oversee 'em, which meant they were getting a lot of free coffee and some godawful food, but I suppose even Jewel's food's better than working.

This year the sheriff decided as how he was too old, too fat, and too mean, I oughta be the one to marshall the Pioneer Week parade. Which meant, on top of having to wear the silly goddamn costume, I had to ride a horse that afternoon. The last horse I tried to get on, when I wasn't much more than a kid, nipped me on the ass. Me and horses never got along too well after that. Needless to say,

I wasn't looking forward to the parade. Or Pioneer Week in general.

I'd just left the Longbranch Inn where I'd had lunch served to me by my ladylove, Glenda Sue Robinson, who'd snapped at me about something I did sometime that pissed her off. Needless to say, I had no idea what she was talking about but apologized anyway. That's what you do with women. Apologize. When that doesn't work, apologize some more. Anyway, that had made my piss-poor mood a little darker than it had already been, so that when I was walking out to my unmarked squad car and happened to glance over to Meechem's Western Wear, which was diagonal across the street from the Longbranch, I almost didn't pay any attention to what I saw.

But when you been a peace officer for getting close to twenty years, you notice little things. Like an old beat-up car pulled up close to the front door, the motor running, and one guy behind the wheel. 'Course it could mean Mindy Sue forgot her fringed leather skirt till the last minute and Buster Lee brought her by real quicklike before the parade. But somehow I doubted it. Meechem's did more business around Pioneer Week than they did the whole year put together, and if I had a criminal bent to my mind, I suppose I might think about hitting on Meechem's myself. So I wandered on over to the Meechem's parking lot to get me a look-see.

The guy behind the wheel was typical Oklahoma redneck, which we seem to have an abundance of here in the heart of Oklahoma. He was wearing a black-net gimme cap, a dirty red T-shirt, and his hair was long, stringy, and sorta brown. The car was, like I said, beat-up looking. A Dodge Charger that had seen better days. The paint was two shades of orange with primer accents, and, I noticed right off, there was mud covering the license plates. Now I've seen "Miami Vice" enough to know what that means.

I was contemplating going over and having a talk with the driver when two guys in ski masks come running out of the front door carrying bags and great big old guns. Big 'uns. So I got out one of my six-shooters, got down in my crouch, pointing the gun like I learned at the academy lo' those many years ago, and yelled, "Sheriff! Freeze!"

The guy driving took off like a son of a bitch, leaving his two buddies and the loot. The two guys in ski masks looked at the car, looked at me, and commenced to shooting. Well, I ducked down beside a Blazer that, until that minute, had a real snazzy paint job.

The only time I'd ever fired the fancy six-shooters we had to wear during Pioneer Week was ten years ago when we first got 'em. I qualify all the goddamn time with my own .45, but who'd think I'd have to fire those damn things? Well, I took aim, squeezed off, and blew the window out of a Chrysler ten feet to the left of the guy I was aiming for. They returned fire, busting out the windshield of the Blazer a little to the right of my favorite ear.

I hit the ground and rolled under the Blazer, which, thank the good Lord, has plenty of ground clearance for a slightly pudgy, slow-moving, middle-aged fella like myself.

Well, the two guys thought they had me on the run, which, of course, they did most certainly not. I was only taking a breather. Figuring my options, so to speak. Then out of nowhere, one of the marked sheriff's cars screeches in, slides to a stop slantways in front of the two perps, and Dalton Pettigrew, one of the day deputies, jumps out, shotgun in hand, and yells, "Stop it now! Y'all just stop!"

Now I may have mentioned that I was in costume for Pioneer Week. I want you to know that even though this is true, I did it in the best possible taste. My Western shirt was of a beige tone, very sedate; my hat was regulation "cowboy" and white (since I'm one of the good guys); and the chaps that covered my Levi's were plain brown leather.

Dalton, on the other hand, was wearing a lime green and yellow Western shirt, his hat was of the ten-gallon variety, and his chaps were sheepskin, the fuzzy kind. The two perps took one look at six-foot-four-inch, two-hundred-and-eighty-pound Dalton in his clown suit and twelve-gauge and dropped their weapons, holding up their hands pretty as you please.

I crawled out from under the Blazer, wondering if I could get the owner to pay for the dry-cleaning of my Western shirt due to the great big old oil stain on the front, but then, looking at the shape of the Blazer, I decided not to argue the point. That's when I heard the sirens, and the other two patrol cars pulled up along with one city car, being as this was their jurisdiction in the first place.

The city police took over the perps, and Dalton walked on over to me. "Hey, Milt, you okay?" he asked, his big, stupid face all concerned.

"Just fine, Dalton. Just fine."

"Milt, I sure am sorry I forgot to turn on my sirene. I heard the call on the radio, and I got so excited, I plumb forgot."

Me, I figure if Dalton had gone by the book and had had his sirens blazing, I'd probably be dead. But if I told Dalton that, he'd never run his goddamn siren for anything, so I just said, "That's okay this time. I won't tell the sheriff."

Dalton gave me a great big old bear hug, and I swear to God there was a tear in his eye when he said, "Thanks, Milt. I owe ya. I really do."

After we got everybody settled down at Meechem's, me and Dalton tooled on over to the County Courthouse in the middle of town, what used to house the Sheriff's Department till we got our own building outside of town. Me and Dalton had papers to fill out, statements to sign, and I figured if I milked it a bit, me being an eyewitness and all, I could be stuck at the police station till late afternoon. Which meant calling the sheriff and telling him how I wouldn't be able to marshall the parade after all.

"Goddamn you, Milt!" Elberry Blankenship yelled into the phone.

"Well, Sheriff," I said, giving it my best whiny, aw-shucks voice, "I can't do nothing about this. I'm real sorry."

"I just bet your red ass you're sorry! I'll get you for this!"

"Yes, sir, I suppose you will."

"You be on night duty till the cows come home, boy."

"If that's what you want, Sheriff."

"Shit." And he hung up. I smiled what my ex-wife called my "shit-eatin' grin" and replaced the receiver. Then I went about signing my statement, which took all of five minutes. Then, of course, I had to meet with the city attorney (because the shoot-out was in city jurisdiction) and the county attorney (because I'm a county employee) and explain why I felt compelled to fire a weapon in defense of my frail, pink body. Since nobody was dead, or even wounded, the meeting took only another fifteen minutes.

After I left the city attorney's office, I went down to the basement where the jail cells are to have me a look-see at the two young fellas that had been shooting at me. I figured it was my right. They had already made themselves to home down there, laying down on their bunks, staring up at the years ahead of them.

"Hey, Doyle," I said to the one I knew, Doyle Kretcher, a homegrown boy. Doyle was one of the middle boys of Rochelle Kretcher, a lady who went to my church. A nice lady with just too many kids and not enough husband.

Doyle looked at me, then looked away. "Hey, boy, I'm talking to you."

Finally, he looked up. "What?"

"Your mama know where you are?"

That's when Doyle spit on the floor and I turned around and left. Wasn't my job to tell his mama. That was gonna be city jurisdiction, not county. I went back upstairs and looked at the rap sheets of the two. Doyle was a nickel and dimer, a skinny, rat-faced little fart, now nineteen and able to do hard time, who'd already been arrested twice. But those charges had been dropped because he was a juvenile and because people basically liked Rochelle Kretcher. But this was big time now. Armed robbery and attempted murder of a peace officer. Namely me.

The other boy was older by two years and had already done some hard time down in Texas at their Huntsville facility. Leave it to a Texan to come up here and botch things up. His name was Lamar Bass and he'd spent two years in Huntsville on a B&E and had been arrested three times before, but the charges had been dropped. So, doing all that, looking at them boys and checking out their rap sheets, took another fifteen minutes.

But, of course, being in the police station necessitated my chewing the fat for a while with my old buddy, Emmett Hopkins, chief of police of Longbranch, which is the county seat of Prophesy County. I went into his office and shook hands, then sat myself down on one of his spindly legged visitor chairs.

Emmett grinned real big and said, "Well, hey there, cowpoke."

I had temporarily forgotten about my getup. "Oh, this," I said, looking sheepishly at my chaps and six-guns and wondering why Emmett was dressed in his usual J.C. Penney's stay-press. "Not my idea."

He shook his head. "Pioneer Week. What a bitch, huh?"

I nodded in the affirmative. "Ain't that the truth?"

"So, how's Miss Jewel Anne doing?" he said, asking after my sister.

"Fine. Just fine. You know she's been going around with Harmon Monk?"

"That's what I hear. Could do worse."

"That's not what my old daddy thought."

"Harmon's changed over the years, Milt. Hell, he's one of the richest men in the county now."

"I know that. I know that."

"And nobody around here begrudges Jewel Anne about Harmon's divorce neither. Leona Monk never was too popular around here. According to Shirley Beth, all she ever did at the Garden Club meetings was talk about how much better the Garden Club was in Oklahoma City. And bitch about how here girls weren't getting a proper education in Bishop like they woulda in the city. Hell, Milt, people were tickled pink when Harmon dumped Leona for Jewel Anne. Even the Catholics.''

"I know that.''

"And everybody knows Harmon's been carrying a torch for Jewel Anne for twenty years or so. Hell, it's plumb romantic. Leastwise, that's what the wife thinks.''

"How's Shirley Beth doing?'' I asked, by way of changing the conversation.

Emmett shrugged. "She's got her good days and her bad days,'' he said. Shirley Beth had taken to drink shortly after her and Emmett lost their boy to leukemia fifteen years before. Everybody knew it, but I don't know anybody who's ever actually seen her drunk. Shirley Beth had always been a lady, and I suppose she thought those things were best kept behind closed doors. Some Sundays she didn't make it to church, and she's missed a Garden Club meeting on more than one occasion, but the gossiping has always been kept to a minimum, and most people just try to act like it's not there. Every year though, she just gets skinnier and skinnier till, pretty soon, I suppose she's just gonna blow away. Sometimes I think Emmett should get her a counselor or something. But that's his business, not mine.

"Hear you're building a pool out to your place," Emmett said.

I nodded. "Damned expensive, too. But when the tornado tore down the stable and corral right after I'd promised Jewel's kids horses, I up and promised them a pool. In the heat of the moment. Now I'm stuck."

"Jewel Anne picking up the tab?" he asked.

I bristled. I didn't like that. Didn't like the implication. Even if the answer was yes. Which it was. "She's paying her part," I answered. "You and Shirley Beth gonna have to come out when it's finished. Sacrifice some chickens to the barbecue and have a swim."

Emmett nodded. "Sounds fine," he said, though I knew it would never happen. Hard to make plans with Shirley Beth's problems.

"You still seeing Glenda Sue?" he asked.

I nodded and grinned. "As often and as much of her as possible."

Emmett laughed. "You're a dirty old man, Milt."

I sighed. "Used to be a dirty young man."

"Didn't we all?"

I stood and Emmett and I shook hands, and I wandered out to my unmarked squad car and drove out of town, finding a nice tree to park under and wait for the proper time to show my face back at the station. Besides, I had a lot to think about. Like just how I felt about having my shiny ass saved by Dalton Pettigrew. Poor, old, pitiful Dalton who's been the butt end of my jokes for several years now. And here he went and practically saved my life. Well, maybe more than practically. I'da felt real bad if I didn't know the whole damn thing had been an accident.

I got back to town at the tail end of the parade and sat in my unmarked squad car at the corner of Main and Crosby and waited for the thing to end. I could hear the high school marching band closer to the front and thanked the good Lord I'd missed that. Even if my nephew Leonard was playing his French horn. I watched the Rebeccas pass by, twenty-three ladies in long evening gowns doing precision marching, and not a one of 'em under sixty. Then came the Masons followed by the Eastern Star and then the Patriots for a Free America, a new group I didn't know much about, about thirty of 'em, all men, all dressed in black slacks, white shirts, and blue gimme hats, marching in step like a well-oiled machine. They were followed by one of the city patrolmen on horseback, signaling the end of the parade. I started up the car and drove on to the station.

Well, Pioneer Week went the way of all Pioneer Weeks. Neil Bob Barnett from Bishop won the hog-calling contest for the tenth year in a row, and a little girl from the south end of the county won first prize for her Angus steer, then cried all over it when she had to give it up to Maynard Dabney, owner of the Longbranch Inn, who always bought the prized steers during Pioneer Week and served 'em for several months after.

On Friday, Emmett Hopkins called me on the phone and asked me if I could come on over to the police station. The two perps from the day before were making bail, and he wanted to know if I wanted to have a little interview with them, with him present of course, before they blew town, which we both knew, and the judge shoulda known, they were gonna do. I said hell yes and hotfooted it over to the courthouse.

By the time I got there, Doyle Kretcher and Lamar Bass were already waiting for me in an interview room, cigarettes hanging out of their mouths and feet up on the table. When Emmett and me walked in there, Emmett whacked Lamar Bass on the legs, knocking his feet off the table and his ass almost to the floor. I grinned. Lamar Bass didn't seem to find the humor in the occasion. Doyle, getting the message, put his feet down and snuffed out the cigarette.

"Whatju want, Deputy?" he sneered in my direction. "Our lawyer's on his way over here to let us out of this hellhole, so be quick about it."

I laughed. "Doyle," I said, "this is a big old courthouse, ya know? And I've heard tell of prisoners being lost in this place for years with their lawyers roaming the halls going, 'Here, boy, here!'"

"You don't go messing with me, Deputy!" Lamar Bass said. "You don't know who the fuck you're messing with."

"Yeah, I do," I said. "Just plain old ordinary Texas white trash."

If possible, Lamar Bass was skinnier, uglier, and more rat-faced than Doyle Kretcher, with beady little eyes that looked two directions at once and made you a bit disoriented. So it was kinda comical to see him try to square his shoulders and stick out his scrawny chest.

"The name Bass mean anything to you?" he said.

"Yeah. It's a big-mouthed, ugly bottom-feeder."

On his fingers he started counting out. "Well, I'll have you know, my great, great, great, great uncle was Sam Bass."

I grinned. "Come from a long line of Texas white trash, do ya? Your mama must be proud."

At this point he jumped up and shouted, "And I'm meaner than Uncle Sam ever thought about being, so you best watch your fucking mouth!"

Emmett put a heavy hand on my shoulder. "Where you two boys gonna be staying while you're out on bail?" he asked.

"My mama's," Doyle mumbled under his breath.

"Your mama put up the bail for you two?" I asked.

Doyle looked at Emmett. "We don't gotta answer that, do we?"

Emmett shook his head. "No, boy, you don't. But you do gotta be at your mama's anytime I decide to check up on you two. Which could be every fifteen minutes or so."

"That's police harassment!" Sam Bass's legacy piped in.

"No, now son," Emmett said, "that's just puredee concern."

Then the door opened and a lawyer I knew from over in Tejas County came in with the bail papers and handed them to Emmett. We watched the two swagger out, then Emmett turned to me and said, "Last we'll see of those two."

I nodded my head in agreement. But we were both wrong.

That night me and Glenda Sue went to the rodeo, which was the climax of Pioneer Week. At the end there was this little ceremony in honor of the Berlin Wall coming down, and I got so emotional I did a dumb thing and asked Glenda Sue to marry me. She didn't spit in my face. But that's about all.

"I been married," she said.

"I know that. So have I."

"Well, don't you think being dumb once is enough?"

"Well, you're not like LaDonna and I sure as hell ain't Linn. Our marriage would be different."

"I don't want to talk about it."

"Why not?"

"Because."

Well, that's about the way it went. When I took her home to her trailer house, she didn't even invite me in, which was definitely not usual because Friday night was always our night for a little loving. Sometimes on Wednesdays, but always on Fridays.

"Aren't you gonna invite me in?" I asked as she got out of the car and bolted for the door of the trailer.

"Not tonight," she said. She didn't add, "I have a headache," which I was not the least bit thankful for. Any excuse would have been better than none at all.

I said, "Glenda Sue!" but nobody heard me 'cause the door was already closed.

You'd think I'd learn. Asking women to marry me has never worked out well. The first one said "yes," then less than twenty years later decided "no" would have been the proper answer. She's getting married again, LaDonna, my ex-wife, is. At Christmas. To Dwayne Dickey, president of the bank. He's an asshole. And not just because he's marrying my ex-wife. He's been an asshole long as I've known him. A woman told me once that it's improper to call a woman an asshole. She said only a man can be an asshole. Sometimes I think she's probably right. All the assholes I've ever known have been men.

The second time I asked a woman to marry me, well, that turned out to be a disaster, too. Maybe it had something to do with her being married at the time. Women can be so goddamn picky.

And now here I was, doing it again. With the same result. I couldn't even get laid.

I took one last look at the trailer—watching the lights go out one by one as Glenda Sue readied herself for bed—put the car in gear, and drove on back to my mountain where my house is, up Mountain Falls Road, snuck up the stairs to my room, and tried to get some sleep.

TWO

I WAS IN a big empty building with cobblestone floors. The only sound I could hear was my shoes tapping as I walked through empty, cavernous space. It seemed to go on forever, that walk. Then I came to an escalator. Only one. Going up. I stepped on. The thing was going real slow, and now there was no sound at all, not even the whir of the machinery moving the escalator.

But as I looked up to the floor above me, I could see a little kid standing at the top of the escalator. A little boy. Looked like one of them kids in the motel room paintings. Great big eyes. Looking down at me. Sad eyes. I wanted to say something. Tell the kid to stay there, not to move. I'd be right there. But I couldn't speak. And the escalator moved so slow, and I couldn't climb it like stairs. I don't know why, but I couldn't.

Then I saw these feet, woman feet, in Red Cross shoes, and calves with leg braces on 'em, and the hem of a skirt. Standing next to the little kid. And I was terrified. More scared than I'd ever been. And I had no idea why.

The little kid looked up and a hand reached down. The little kid took the hand, looked back at me once, then turned and walked away, the woman legs moving stiffly next to him. Then my voice came. I screamed, "No!"

And woke myself up. I was sweating like a son of a bitch. A cold, clammy sweat. And shaking all over. I got up and went to the bathroom, took a piss, and rinsed my face with cold water. I went back to my room, changing out of my T-shirt and shorts, which were drenched in sweat. I put on fresh and took a beer out of my little icebox and found a piece of leftover pizza. I took the beer and pizza back to the bed and sat there with the light on, chasing away the devil and wishing for a cigarette. I hadn't had one in twenty years and hadn't wanted one in ten, but, God almighty, did I want one now. The nearest store was eighteen miles away. Jewel Anne didn't smoke, and none of the kids did to my knowledge.

I got up and slipped down the hall to the room my two nephews, Leonard and Carl, now shared, since Leonard's private apartment over the garage got blown away in the tornado, along with the garage. I went on little cat's feet to Leonard's bed and shook him awake.

"Whaa..." he said.

"You got a cigarette?" I asked in a whisper.

"What?"

"A cigarette. You got one?"

"Jesus. I don't smoke."

"That's okay if you do. I don't mind. I just want one if you have one."

"I don't smoke! And neither do you! Don't you know those things'll kill you?"

"That's okay. I don't mind. You don't have one, huh?"

"No!" he said, loud enough to wake up Carl, if Carl were a normal human being and actually woke up to things like loud noises, houses catching on fire, tornadoes, stuff like that.

Leonard turned his back on me, and I moved out of his room and back to mine, finally falling asleep with the light on.

The next morning I woke up later than usual and went downstairs. The kids had already eaten and were outside doing chores. Jewel Anne was in the kitchen, clearing the breakfast dishes.

"Well, it's about time you woke up," she said.

"Um," I said.

"You hungry?" she said.

"Um," I said.

"What in the world were you doing waking up Leonard last night asking for a cigarette?"

"What?"

"Last night. You woke up Leonard and asked for a cigarette."

"No, I didn't."

"He said you did."

"He must have been dreaming."

"Um," she said.

And that's when it happened. The phone rang. One minute life was okay, maybe not wonderful, but okay. And then the phone rang, and life wasn't okay anymore. And maybe never would be again.

Jewel answered it, then handed it to me. "It's the sheriff," she said.

I wasn't on duty that weekend, at least I hadn't been before I neglected to marshall the parade, and I didn't know if the sheriff had changed the schedule without telling me. Gingerly, I took the phone.

"Hey, Sheriff," I said.

"Milton." There was a silence.

"Yes, sir?" I又 said.

"Milton, boy, I got some bad news."

"Yes, sir?" A wreck on the highway? His mama? His wife?

"Milton, it's Glenda Sue. There's no way to say it but just to say it. Boy, she's dead."

I sat down heavily on a kitchen chair. "Elberry..."

"You see her last night?"

"Yeah . . ."

"What time you leave her place?"

"What happened? She can't be dead... What happened?"

"Somebody kilt her, boy."

"Jesus... Jesus... God..."

"What time you leave her place, Milt?"

"Ah...after...the rodeo. I didn't stay. I left right after I took her home. She was mad. She didn't ask me in. Was somebody in there? Elberry?"

"You two have a fight?"

"What? No. I asked her to marry me."

"And she got mad?"

"Yes, sir. Women do that." I gulped in air. There didn't seem to be enough air. Not enough to breathe properly. "Where is she, Elberry? I want to see her. Where is she?"

"No, boy, you don't want to see her."

I stood up, my hand so tight on the phone I could feel the plastic bending. "I want to see her! Goddamn it! I gotta see her!"

Elberry's voice was soft. So soft I had to strain to hear the words. "She was messed up bad, Milton. Somebody messed her up real bad before they put her out of her misery."

"Oh, Jesus. Sweet Jesus." The tears were running freely down my face. I could feel Jewel's hands on my back, rubbing my shoulders, my neck. I handed the phone to her and tore out to the car.

I don't remember getting in the car, starting it, driving the eighteen miles to Longbranch, going into the Longbranch Memorial Hospital, screaming at Dr. Jim's assistant. I don't remember any of that. All I remember is the sight of Glenda Sue when he pulled back the green sheet. There was a large gap where her pretty, long neck had been. Her face was puffy and bruised, and there were cigarette burns on her breasts, thighs, and feet. Two fingers were missing. I sat down on the cold, antiseptic floor and cried. Dr. Jim's assistant tried to pick me up, but I hit him. He moved Glenda Sue back into cold storage and left me sitting there on the floor crying.

I'm not sure how long it was before Elberry showed up. Him and Dalton. Dalton picked me up in his arms like a baby and carried me out of the morgue. I remember putting my head on his shoulder and crying. He stood me up in the hallway outside and leaned me against the wall. I knew all this was happening, but I really didn't care. I hurt. All over. Like I've never hurt before. I been beat up. In the Air Force once, I was even shot. Accidentally. It didn't hurt like this. The all over body ache worse than any flu known to the world.

"What time you get home last night?" Elberry asked.

"I don't know."

"Think."

I shook my head. It was full of cobwebs. And worms. And other nasty crawly things. "Ten-thirty. Eleven. I don't know."

"Jewel Anne see you? The kids?"

"No, I don't think so." Then, through all the little nasties crawling through my head, it dawned on me. "Jesus Christ." I looked up at Elberry. "You think I did this? *Me?*"

Elberry shook his head. "No, boy, I know you didn't. I know you. But the county attorney's gonna look at you first. You were the last to see her alive."

"Fuck!" I took a swing at Elberry, but Dalton blocked it with one of his big fists.

He shook his sad, stupid face. "Now don't be doing that, Milt."

I shook myself. "I gotta..." I started, then wondered what I had been about to say. I gotta what? Go someplace? Do something? Die? I didn't know. I leaned up against the wall again. "Jesus Christ," I whispered, half to myself.

"You know where Linn Robinson is?" the sheriff asked me. Linn was Glenda Sue's ex-husband. My former best friend. While they were married he'd used pretty Glenda Sue as a punching bag on a regular basis.

I shook my head. "Last I heard he got religion and got married. Ardmore, I think. I don't know."

"Off the sauce?"

"Yeah."

"So what if he got back on? His new wife leaves him, and he figures all his troubles are Glenda Sue's fault. He comes back here..."

I shrugged. I didn't care. What good would it do? It wouldn't take away what she had gone through in her last minutes of life. It wouldn't stop that.

"She had a kid, right?" Elberry asked.

I nodded.

"Where is she? The kid?"

I shrugged. "I don't know. Glenda Sue never talked about her. I haven't seen her since she went off to OU, ten, fifteen years ago."

"She needs to be notified."

"Yeah. Hey, kid, your mama's dead. You should see her, what a mess!"

Elberry and Dalton just looked at me, Dalton finally turning away, unable to look at the mess that was me.

The sheriff shrugged. "Should be something in the trailer will tell us where the kid is." Turning to Dalton, he said. "Take Milt on home. Him and

Jewel can come back later and get his car. He shouldn't be driving." And to me he said, "You're off duty, as of this minute. You ain't in this, you understand?"

"Fuck you," I said and strode off down the hall on shaky legs. Dalton, close behind me, kept trying to grab my arm. I kept pulling away. Finally, outside, right near my cherry '55 Chevy Belaire, Dalton caught me.

"Sheriff wants me to drive you home, Milt," he said, real gentlelike. Like talking to an invalid or some old person with one foot in the grave.

"Fuck the sheriff," I said, "and fuck you, too."

"Now, Milt . . ."

I pulled away and got in my '55, started the engine, and burned rubber getting out of my parking space. I drove straight to Glenda Sue's trailer.

There was yellow tape around the door of the trailer, and Mike Neils, the other day deputy, was sitting in a squad car in the yard. I pulled in and braked, followed close behind by Dalton. We got out of our cars at the same time, but I was to the door and ripping off the tape before Dalton could react.

"Now, Milt, I know the Sheriff wouldn't like that."

I didn't say anything. Just opened the door and went in. Glenda Sue's trailer was a little, two-

bedroom singlewide. One room served as kitchen
and living room. A short hall led to a dinky little
bedroom, then a bathroom so tiny you had to stand
in the hall to take a piss, and ended at the master
bedroom, which was just about big enough for a
double bed and small dresser. Glenda Sue had
crammed the whole trailer full of furniture. Way
too much furniture. And she collected cacti. I'd
had more than one prickly pear up my ass while
spending time with my lady.

The rocking chair we'd bought together at a garage sale over in Bishop was turned upside down.
The wagon wheel coffee table was turned over, the
glass on top broken. And there was blood all over
the Early American print couch. The smell of
blood and burned flesh hung in the air like a visi-
ble, living thing.

And Glenda Sue wasn't there. Would never be
there again. Would never yell at me for leaving
socks on the dining table again. Would never laugh
at my silly jokes again. Would never touch me in
that special way again. Glenda Sue wasn't there.
She was laying on a cold metal tray in Dr. Jim's
morgue, getting ready to be cut up some more.

"Come on now, Milt," I heard Dalton say.
"Let's get us on out of here."

"Yeah, Milt," Mike Neils said softly. "This is
no place for you to be. Come on."

I turned to my two deputies. The two men who worked under me, followed my orders, listened to me. The voice that came out of me was one even I didn't recognize. I just said softly, oh, so softly, "Y'all go on. Just go on outside. Leave me alone."

They looked at each other, then left, shutting the trailer door behind them, leaving me alone in a place I'd never been alone in before.

"Hey, Milt, what are you doing here?"

I look up. Shit, Glenda Sue. "Eating," I say.

"Whatsa matter? LaDonna kick you out?" she says, grinning down at me.

"As a matter of fact, yes."

Her grin fades and she sits down at my table, her white waitress uniform tucked under her, her order pad lying on the Formica tabletop.

"Shit, Milt, I'm sorry, I didn't know..."

I pat her hand and quickly pull my hand back. "That's okay. Nobody much knows about it. Actually, she'd didn't kick me out. She just left. Last week. I been eating tuna and peanut butter for a week. Figured I could use some real food."

"Well, you got it, Milt. And it's on the house."

"No, now, Glenda Sue..."

"Chicken-fried steak? Sound good?"

I smile. "Sounds great."

The food keeps coming, and every time she brings something out, she sits down for a spell. It's a Wednesday night, and the Longbranch is near empty.

"You get through it, you know. I did," she says.

"Yeah, I know."

"Just takes time."

I nod my head.

I finish my food and stand up, looking for my check. As I'm looking, she comes out of the back room, dressed in her street clothes, a purse over her arm.

"Whatja looking for?"

"My ticket."

Glenda Sue grins. "Like I told you, it's on the house."

I shake my head. "I can't let you do that ..."

"Tell you what, I could use a ride home. How's that?"

I drive her out to her trailer. The night's black, no moon, just stars sprinkled across the sky like lights on a Christmas tree.

"I got a six-pack of Bud in the icebox with your name on it," she says.

"No kidding?" I say. "Got my name right on it?"

"Says 'Milt' big as shit."

I get out and follow her into the trailer. She pops the tops on two cold ones, and we sit down on the sofa, Glenda Sue kicking off her shoes.

"Life's a bitch, Milt," she says.

"That's what they tell me," I say, stretching my legs out under the coffee table, "and I ain't got anything to prove 'em wrong." I take a sip of my beer. "How's that girl of yours, Melissa?"

Glenda Sue shrugs. "Up at OU. Getting too smart for her britches." She glances over at me. "You wanna take off that jacket? It's kinda warm in here."

"Thanks," I say, shrugging out of my suit coat I've had on since work that day.

"I sure am sorry about you and LaDonna," she says.

I nod.

"But to tell you the truth, Milt, I never did see what you saw in that skinny little prude."

"Hell, Glenda Sue, what could I do? Linn had you."

She smiles at me. "You know, I always sorta figured you had a thing for me."

I can feel myself turning red. "Since the sixth grade."

Her hand reaches out and undoes the top button of my shirt. "I think LaDonna was an idiot for letting you loose."

"Me too," I say, reaching for her.

The next morning, while Glenda Sue sleeps, I sneak out of bed and put on my clothes, all but my

*shoes, and tiptoe out the front door. Start my car
and leave.*

There was a little Formica-covered desk in a
corner of the kitchen. I went over to it. That was
where Glenda Sue kept her correspondence, bills,
stuff like that. I sat down in the little desk chair
with the red-and-blue cushion tied on to the legs
and back, and opened the drawer.

There was a Christmas card from last year from
her Aunt Ida, her mama's sister over in North
Carolina, dated three weeks after Christmas; a
couple of bills that wouldn't come due for another
two weeks or more; a little rubber-banded package
of bill receipts; some pens and pencils; batteries;
road maps; emery board and cuticle gunk; a picture album I'd never seen with pictures of her and
Linn and the baby, either early on when they were
still happy or in between bouts of Linn's terror;
and way in the back, under a box of stationery, I
found a letter from Melissa, Glenda Sue's daughter. The envelope had a return address in California and was postmarked about five months back.
I didn't read the letter, just took the envelope over
to the phone and called information for Oakland,
California.

THREE

I THINK MAYBE funerals were invented to keep the bereaved busy. 'Cause I sure as hell was. Floyd Ackerman, over at Ackerman's Funeral Home, was real good, helped me a lot with the planning of it. But I was moving on not too much juice. That Saturday night, and the following Sunday night, whenever I tried to sleep, that same dream would come to me. The one about the little kid and the woman legs. I didn't know why I was dreaming that dream instead of one about Glenda Sue, but it was bothersome just the same. I spent both nights staring out the many windows of my upstairs room, counting leaves falling from the trees.

"Do you want a notice telling the mourners not to send flowers?" Floyd Ackerman asked me. "A lot of people are doing that now-a-days. Having the money sent to a favorite charity."

I thought about that for a minute.

"What is it?" I ask.

"A corsage, dumbass," Glenda Sue says. "Ain't it pretty?"

"Why'd Linn send you a corsage?"

"'Cause he wants me to go to the dance with him, idiot.''

"To the dance?"

"Yeah. You know, dummy, the school dance?"

"Oh. You going?"

She gazed at the corsage, a stupid, sappy look on her face.

"I guess so," she finally says, then sighs, "I ain't never had nobody send me flowers before. Pretty, huh?"

"No, I don't want any notice," I told Floyd. "Flowers would be nice."

Monday, Melissa Sue Robinson flew in from California. Being smart enough to know when I haven't got all my wits about me, I planned on having Leonard drive me to Tulsa to pick up the girl. On the way I had him drive me to the courthouse, where I went in to see Emmett Hopkins.

He stood up and gripped me on the arm. "Milt . . . Milt . . ."

I nodded my head and so did he as he let go of my arm and just stood there. Finally, I cleared my throat. "Emmett, them two boys, the Kretcher boy and the other one . . ."

Emmett nodded. "I thought of them as soon as I heard. Went straight over to Mrs. Kretcher's. But them boys ain't there. Accordingly to her, they never even showed up. Looks like they hightailed it right out of town from here.''

"Unless they stuck around long enough to make a little stop in the country that night.''

Emmett shook his head. ''I don't know. I just don't know. But I put the word out on them two. Every department in the state. We'll find 'em.''

I shook his hand. ''Let me know when you do.''

He didn't answer. Just looked at me like maybe I thought he was stupid or something.

I went outside and got back in the '55 and had Leonard drive me on to Tulsa.

We got to the airport in plenty of time to park the car, get to the gate, and wait. Fifteen minutes later the doors opened and Melissa Sue Robinson's flight deplaned. I recognized the girl right off the bat. 'Course, Melissa wasn't so much a girl anymore. Nudging thirty like a son of a bitch. From the wrong side. But knowing Glenda Sue got herself knocked up shortly after graduation, it figured the girl would be that old.

And Lord, did she look like her mama. Fair and blond. Littler than Glenda Sue. Maybe only five foot two. Tiny figure. Looked younger really than what she was. Pretty face. Dressed in blue jeans and a fluffy pink sweater. And hanging off one arm was a surprise. A little girl, no more than five years old, wearing red pants and a Mickey Mouse sweatshirt, with big black eyes, dark kinky-curly hair, and what must have been her father's complexion. Glenda Sue had never mentioned a grandbaby, and I hate to think her reason was that the baby's daddy had been of the colored persuasion. Or maybe there was some other reason. Like maybe she didn't know.

I walked up to Melissa and held out my hand. "Melissa, I'm..."

She smiled. "Deputy Kovak. I remember you. You used to come out to the trailer when Daddy beat up Mama."

Well, nothing shy about this girl. "That's right," I said, trying to return her smile.

She touched my arm with her small hand. "This must be very difficult for you."

I only nodded. Looking over at Leonard, getting ready to tell him to go get their bags, I noticed the boy's mouth was hanging open. Looked like it finally happened—Leonard was in love.

"This is my nephew, Leonard Hotchkiss," I said.

Melissa smiled. "Hi, Leonard."

Leonard's face began to melt. His eyeballs bugged out and a little bit of spit dribbled down his chin. Ain't love grand?

"Got your baggage claim?" I asked, holding my hand out. She gave it to me, and I handed it to

Leonard. "Go on now, boy," I said, giving him a little push to get him started. After Leonard had left, I looked down at the child still holding tightly to Melissa's hand. "And who's this?"

Melissa's smile got larger than ever. "My daughter, Rebecca. Rebecca, say hello to Deputy Kovak."

The little girl smiled, showing a big gap where her two front teeth should have been, and ducked her head behind Melissa's leg, letting only one Mickey ear peek out. "Well, hey, Rebecca," I said, not being too all-fired good around kids. I like 'em best when they're old enough to look you in the eye and tell you to go squat. I can deal with that. Looking back at Melissa, I said, "Well, now, maybe we best go on out to the car."

Which we did. I drove around the parking lot and out, paying my fair share of the Tulsa city taxes to ransom my car, and moved around to the white zone in front of the baggage area where Leonard was waiting—with five bags. Three big ones and two little ones. A lot more baggage than I had anticipated.

"Gonna stay for a while?" I said to Melissa as she and Leonard and I packed the trunk.

"This is everything Rebecca and I own," the girl said cheerfully. "Reagan cutbacks canceled my job a few months ago, and I was fighting an eviction notice when I got your call, so I just said screw it, packed up, and left. All the furniture's just Goodwill specials. I left it.''

"Oh,'' I said. What do you say? I've never been real good about practical total strangers telling me their business. Unless of course it's police business. But that tends to embarrass me a mite, too.

As I shut the trunk and Leonard got in the backseat with Rebecca, Melissa said, ''I take it Mama didn't mention Rebecca to you.''

I cleared my throat. "Well,'' I said, and looked around. ''Well, she mighta, but I don't really remember.''

Melissa laughed. ''You'd remember that. No, I can't see Mama bragging on her grandbaby. She never did approve of Anthony, Rebecca's father.'' She added, as if an afterthought, ''He was black.''

"Oh,'' I said, as if I hadn't figured that out. What do you say?

I got in the car and started the two-hour drive back to Prophesy County, wondering about this girl Melissa.

My first week with the sheriff's office and I have no idea what I'm doing. Sheriff Blankenship says do it, I do it. We only have two day deputies and the sheriff. I'm all alone in the office when the door opens and the little girl runs in.

"He's doing it again!" she pants, out of breath from her four-mile run.

I get up off my chair and look around. "Who's doing what?" I ask.

"My daddy's beating up on my mama again, Deputy! Come on! You gotta stop him!"

She grabs my arm and starts pulling. I lock up the door to the Sheriff's Department and follow the kid to the squad car, noticing she seems to know the ropes, gets right in the car like she's done it all before. She gives me directions, and I drive out to the country, pulling into the dirt road leading up to the little trailer. When I stop the car, I notice the trailer swaying a bit and screams and grunts coming from within. I pull my .45 and tell the little girl to stay in the car.

Gingerly, I walk up to the door, knock, and identify myself. Nobody answers or pays any attention, so I go on in.

Although I've been back in Longbranch for five years, since my discharge from the Air Force, I haven't seen Linn and Glenda Sue since my wedding to LaDonna, right after I got out. I don't even know they're living out here.

When I pull the guy off the woman in the trailer, at first I don't even realize it's them. All it is is a family disturbance, the kind of call every cop's afraid of, and all I know is I have to get the guy to stop. He takes a swing at me, and I grab his arm, pinning it behind him, and thrust him into a chair. That's when I recognize him.

"Linn?"

"Huh?" He's too drunk to focus, his anger still in charge.

I look behind me at the woman lying on the floor, blood on her swollen face. "Glen? That you?"

I bend down and help her sit up.

"Hey, Milt," she says, grinning through the battered face, one tooth missing and bruises already beginning to show, the lips swollen and bloody. Someone I barely recognize as Glenda Sue. "How you doing?" she says.

I slowed the car, finally turning into the road to my house. "I figured it would be better if you stayed with us," I told the grown-up Melissa, "rather than at your mama's trailer. Sheriff's office's not through with it yet." I didn't mention the condition of the place.

My house has nine rooms, most of 'em added as afterthoughts. One, a little room added on sometime after the original house was built, probably at the same time the master bedroom suite was built on the ground floor, connected the dining room and the master bedroom. By the original wallpaper we found three deep in there, the room had originally been a nursery. Jewel Anne and I had been using it as sort of a catchall. There was a little desk in there where Jewel did the bills, an ironing board, and boxes Jewel never got around to unpacking.

We had already moved the boxes into the utility room, and the desk and ironing board into the master bedroom, which was Jewel's. Then we had taken the trundle bed from Marlene's room (she's Jewel's daughter, the middle child) and put it in my room, and moved my double bed to the little room on the ground floor, along with a cardboard chest of drawers that used to house Marlene's dolls' clothes and now held her collection of cute boy magazines. You know those things, whoever's hot this week on some sitcom, they got a hundred eleven pictures of him in various shades of unattire. So anyway, we had the room all ready.

"I don't want to put you out," Melissa said to my invitation.

"No problem. Everything's all set up."

We pulled up in front of the house, and I honked the horn. Jewel, Marlene, and Carl came out to meet us. Jewel went ape-shit when she saw Rebecca. The girl's always had this thing about little kids.

Leonard, Carl, and I got the bags in while Jewel took Melissa and Rebecca into the kitchen and fed 'em. Poor things. It took another hour before Melissa and I were alone, sitting in the living room, the kids outside showing Rebecca what Oklahoma looked like and Jewel Anne off somewheres trying to be out of the way.

"So," Melissa said. "You said Mama was killed. You want to elaborate?"

"No." I shook my head. "I mean...hell, I don't know what I mean. Your mama was murdered, Melissa. Somebody did some bad stuff to her."

"You think it was Daddy?"

The girl had a way of getting right to the point.

"I got no way of knowing at this stage of the investigation," I said. "The Sheriff's Department is looking into it."

"Was she beaten?"

"Yes."

"Is that what killed her?"

"No."

"Deputy Kovak..."

"Honey, her throat was cut. That's what killed her."

Melissa shook her head. "Not Daddy then. If she'd been beaten to death, I'd say he'd be a good candidate. But that's not his style."

The girl was beginning to get on my nerves. She'd shown no signs of regret over Glenda Sue. All her statements were matter-of-fact. It was like she was reading something out of a book or watching a made-for-TV movie. Not being able to take it anymore, I said, "This doesn't seem to be bothering you much."

Melissa sighed. "Deputy Kovak, I lost my mother years ago. She's been dead to me for a long time. I've already done my grieving."

"Because of...what was his name? Anthony?"

She shrugged. "That...and other things. She worked her ass off to send me to college, then decided I was too uppity once I got an education. Every time I'd come home, she'd say how I thought I was too good to live in a trailer. Stuff like that."

"That's just a little thing..."

"Little things can become big if they're said often enough. She came to visit me *once* in Norman the whole four years I was in school. She came unannounced early one Saturday morning. Anthony and I were in bed. She took one look at him, turned around, and walked out. It was almost as if she'd been looking for a reason to cut me off entirely.

"For three weeks I tried calling her, but she hung up when she heard my voice. So I went home for a visit. She *did* let me in. I stayed for about two hours. The whole two hours she told me what she thought of me. How she hadn't slaved at the

Longbranch Inn to put me through school for me
to turn into nothing but an 'uppity nigger-lover', as
she put it. So I left.

"When Anthony and I graduated, we moved to
California, where he had a good job offer. I wrote
her and told her my new address. I never heard
from her. When I got pregnant with Rebecca six
years ago, Anthony decided fatherhood wasn't for
him, and he took off. He's never even seen Rebecca. I wrote Mother and told her. Told her I was
pregnant and that Anthony was gone. She sent me
a two word telegram: 'Abort it.'"

I shook my head. Not that I didn't believe her
story, because I did. I knew Glenda Sue real well,
and one thing I knew for sure about her was that
once she got her mind set on something, she didn't
let go of it in an all-fired rush. In a lot of ways,
Glenda Sue was a real good woman. But I guess in
some ways, she was just plain human. She made
mistakes.

"I'm sorry," I said. "Seems like you haven't had
a lot of breaks in your life."

Her blue eyes got big in surprise. "What? Hey,
I'm doing okay. I've got a degree and a profes-
sion. I've got a beautiful, healthy daughter. And,
believe it or not, I had a pretty happy childhood.
And that was all Mama's doing. She was a great
mother until I went off to school. Then I guess her

own insecurities took hold. But when I was younger, even when Daddy lived with us, things were okay. It was Mama and me against the beast. You won't believe this, but we used to laugh at him behind his back. We'd make a game out of coming up with ways to get him when he went after Mama. But when I was twelve, he came into my room one night. There was no doubt in my mind what he was planning, so I screamed for Mama. She came in with that old baseball bat and damn near killed him."

And I guess it was that, remembering her mama from the good days, that finally made it all real. Tears came to her eyes, and she stood up and said, "excuse me," and quickly left the room.

That was okay. 'Cause I was remembering the same woman. The one that shot Linn Robinson full of bird shot every time he came home after that, until he finally left town. Yeah, that was my Glenda Sue. Slow to burn, but when she did, God almighty, watch out.

I sat in the living room, watching the sun slowly go down between the twin peaks over in Tejas County that could be seen from the back of the house. I sat and watched that and listened to the voices of the kids outside. And I thought about how it wasn't real yet. How I could just get up and walk over to the phone in the entry hall and dial

Glenda Sue's number and how she'd answer. Even with Melissa in the house, it still wasn't real.

So far in my life, I'd buried my daddy and my mama and my sister's husband. Daddy had died of a heart attack at sixty-five. A surprise, but still to me he was old. When you're an adult, you expect the death of your parents. Mama had been a long time dying of cancer, and she was in her eighties when it took her. Henry, Jewel's husband, had been shot to death, but it didn't affect me in a personal way, 'cause I never really knew Henry and never particularly cared for him.

But Glenda Sue. Oh, God, Glenda Sue. This was different. I sat and listened to the voices of the children, the tinkling laughter of Glenda Sue's grandbaby, the grandbaby she never let herself know, and I got mad. Mad at Glenda Sue for not letting the child into her life, mad at me for being dumb enough to ask her to marry me and letting her keep me out of her place where maybe I could have saved her, big he-man me. And then it dawned on me that it shouldn't be me or Glenda Sue I was mad at.

Somebody was out there, out there in the great big ol' world around me, who had done that to Glenda Sue. Had taken her life, and before that her dignity. And that somebody was gonna pay, come hell or high water.

FOUR

THE LAST PERSON I expected to see at my girl-friend's funeral was my ex-wife. She and Glenda Sue had never been the best of friends in high school, LaDonna had always been jealous of Glenda Sue, mainly because I'd known Glenda Sue longer and been half in love with her for most of my life. But LaDonna was like that, petty.

Later, while Glenda Sue was having her trouble with Linn, LaDonna was of the opinion that Glenda Sue must have liked being beat up, else why would she stay with him? I never thought that was the reason, but I often wondered why she put up with it for twelve years. But we never know what's in somebody else's head and heart, at least that's what my mama used to say, and it always rang true to me.

But even so, even if she never had liked her, LaDonna was there to bid her farewell. Along with good old Dwayne. But the funeral of the victim of a murder as sensational as Glenda Sue's is a bit of social event anywhere, and Prophesy County was no exception. The place was packed, and I'd bet most of the people there even knew Glenda Sue. I sat in the front row with Melissa and Jewel. The kids stayed home, the big ones watching Rebecca.

Glenda Sue wasn't a church goer, but me and Jewel Anne were, so Reverend Castle of the First Baptist Church of Longbranch officiated as a favor to me. He'd known Glenda Sue, of course, from the Longbranch Inn. Everybody did. She'd worked there for thirty years. He spoke real kindly about her, and said those things preachers always say, about how she was going to a better place and all. I hoped he was right. I hoped she was up in Heaven now with her mama and daddy and that baby she lost two years after Melissa. Having a family reunion. That would be grand.

"What are y'all doing?" the girl asks. *Girls, yuck.*

"We're playing. You go away. Go play with them girls over there," says Linn, *my new best friend since that morning.*

The girl looks over at the pack of other girl playing across the asphalt playground. *"They're doing sissy stuff. You doing anything fun?"*

"Well, we ain't doing sissy stuff," Linn answers. *I keep looking down at the marbles in the circle on the asphalt. I figure, you don't look at one of 'em, maybe they'll just go away.*

"Y'all playing marbles?" the girl asks.

"No we're playing tiddlywinks," Linn answers, and I hoot with laughter. Linn's funny. Real funny.

"Well, y'all got some real sorry-looking marbles there, all I can say," the girl says.

Finally, with the look of superiority I learned from Linn since that morning, I look up. "Why don't you go play with your dolls?" I say.

"Why don't you go jump up a rope?" the girl says.

"You think you know how to play marbles?" Linn asks.

"Better than you."

He thumbs a shooter at her and she catches it in her hand and kneels down on the ground, the pink skirt of her dress caught under her knees. Five minutes later, she has all our marbles.

"You don't play like no girl," Linn says, spitting mad.

"I never said I did," the girl says.

"Why don't you go cut out some paper dolls?" I say, sitting back on my haunches.

"Way you play, maybe you should change to paper dolls." The girl stands up and starts to move away. "Anybody asks you who whopped your butt, you tell 'em Glenda Sue Rainey, hear?"

After the service was concluded, me and Melissa and Reverend Castle stood at the front door and shook hands with everybody as they filed out.

Took almost an hour. People kept saying things to me, but I mostly didn't listen, just nodded my head. I didn't want to hear their words of condolence, afraid I might start bawling at something nice somebody said.

When I saw LaDonna and Dwayne come up, both dressed in funeral black that looked too new to have ever been washed, I thought about jumping in the bushes and hiding, but figured that wouldn't be the dignified thing to do. I owed it to Glenda Sue to give her departure as much class as I had.

"Milton," my ex-wife said, taking my hand.

"LaDonna."

"I'm so sorry."

"Thank you."

I thought about how I felt seeing her again. LaDonna. But decided that was something I'd think about later. Things were bad enough as it was without dragging out my feelings. I try not to do that if I can help it. Which is something every woman I've ever known has bitched about.

Then I felt Dwayne Dickey's hand on my arm, in that way he had of doing, and I bristled all over, trying to remind myself that knocking guests down at funerals is not a classy thing to do.

"God, Milt, what can I say?" Dwayne boomed.

"Nothing," I said to myself.

"LaDonna and I are just so saddened by this turn of events." What an asshole. Didn't I tell you this guy was an asshole? "If there's anything LaDonna and I can do to help, Milt, you just let us know, hear?" And then he slapped me on the back.

"Thank you," I said, turning to the next person.

Who happened to be my boss. Sheriff Elberry Blankenship. "Boy, what can I say?" he said, pumping my hand and looking at the ground. I hadn't seen him since the day Glenda Sue's body had been discovered, later in the evening when he'd come by to pick up my weapon and badge, as I was on temporary leave of absence. I'd gotten pissed and gone upstairs, leaving Jewel Anne to give him what he wanted.

"I need to talk with you, Elberry," I replied.

"Sure, son, anytime."

"Right after the funeral. Your place or the office?"

"Milton . . ." he started, but I didn't let him finish.

"How about the office? Say two o'clock?"

Nadine, the sheriff's wife, was right behind him. She moved Elberry over with a twitch of her hip and kissed me on the cheek. "Forget the office," she said, "you come on over to the house and I'll fix us all some dinner."

I smiled at this lady I'd shared a secret or two with in the past. "Thanks, Mrs. Blankenship. Some other time, though."

She nodded her head in understanding and moved on. I shook hands with just about everybody I knew or had ever known. Bert and Mavis Davis and their daughter, Kathy Ann; Haywood Hunter, an ex-neighbor of mine who was now living in town in a nice little two bedroom he bought with the proceeds of selling his tornado-ruined RV court; Mrs. Eva Jean Horne, my ex-landlady, and her sister, the sheriff's mama; Dalton, Mike, and Jasmine, our deputies, knowing old A.B. Tate must be minding the store while everybody else was at the funeral. I'd have to give him some time off for that. Gladys, our clerk, and her husband, Arvelle. Dr. Jim, the county medical examiner, was there, and, bless his heart, he hadn't made one morbid joke since the whole thing began, letting me know that those morbid jokes of his weren't as unconscious as he'd like you to believe.

I shook hands with all the waitresses at the Longbranch Inn, the restaurant being closed today in honor of Glenda Sue, which I thought was mighty nice, and with the cooks, dishwashers, and busboys. Pulling up the end of the procession of

Longbranch Inn employees was Maynard Dabney, the owner of the place.

"Milt," he said, shaking my hand with one of his while the other grabbed a fistful of my right sleeve. "She was a fine woman." I nodded in agreement. "Best waitress in the place. But she's gonna be missed for more than that. She was a real good person, know what I mean?" Again I nodded my head as he moved on. I wasn't sure how much more I could take.

Finally, the hand shaking was over, and it was time to go to the cemetery. Glenda Sue had had a small insurance policy that covered the cost of the funeral and the burial. She already owned the plot, right next to her mama and daddy and her dead baby at the old Maplewood Cemetery outside of town.

After she was laid to rest, with enough flowers to take her through eternity and beyond, I excused myself from Jewel Anne and Melissa, giving them my car to take back up to Mountain Falls Road where I knew a feast would be laid out, brought by the ladies of the church and others. I hoped there'd be some left by the time I got back and hitched a ride to the station with Dalton and Mike. Jasmine would go on home, as she was on night duty.

The sheriff was in his office, and I went in and shut the door. "You wanted to talk, Milt?" he said, leaning back in his swivel chair as I took one of his two visitor chairs.

"You check into Linn Robinson?" I asked.

"Yeah. You were right: Ardmore. But he's got an alibi thicker than my mama's corn bread. Seems your old buddy Linn done more than just got religion. He's a preacher now. One of them off-the-wall brands. He was giving 'em hell from the pulpit of a tent-meeting revival from six Friday night till noon Saturday. Marathon style. Brought four hundred souls to Jesus, bless his little green heart. And every goddamn one of 'em will swear he was up there sweatin' and cryin' the whole damn time."

"I never did like Linn much for this anyway, Sheriff, truth be known. Not his style."

The sheriff didn't say anything, just sat there rocking back and forth in his swivel chair.

"I wanna come back to work," I finally said.

"Too soon," he said, shaking his head.

"No, sir, it's not. I can't just sit around my house doing nothin'. I wanna find out who did that to Glenda Sue, and I wanna send him to jail."

Elberry leaned forward, resting his arms on his desk. "If jail's what you're thinking about, Milton, that's good. But a man in your position, I surely don't think jail *is* what you're thinking about. I think you're thinking about how you could just blow this guy away once you find out who it is. How maybe you might just save the tax-payers some money. You thought about that any?''

I nodded my head. ''I'd be lying if I said I hadn't thought that. But that's not really me, Elberry, and you know it. I wanna work. I gotta work.''

Elberry nodded his head and opened his desk drawer, taking out my badge and gun. He shoved them across the desk to me. ''Welcome home,'' he said.

MY FIRST official act was to go back to Glenda Sue's place. The state police had come in to take fingerprints for us, which is what we do, not having a forensics team of our own, and the yellow tape had been taken off Glenda Sue's door that morning before the funeral. It must have been sometime during the funeral that the damage had been done. The place had been trashed, and not by burglars, either. Glenda Sue's nineteen-inch Sony still sat on the shelf by the bed, just like it always had, except the back had been taken off and the innards smashed. Just like everything else in the trailer. The sofa had been ripped open with a butcher knife, the stuffing everywhere. Everything in the refrigerator had been dumped on the floor, jars opened and contents spilled. The mattress on the bed was ripped open, and even the little toilet had been pulled up from the floor.

There was nothing inheritable left in the place for Melissa and her baby.

The thought crossed my mind that somebody was looking for something. That maybe the torture of my ladylove hadn't just been somebody's idea of a good time, but a methodical way of finding something out. But what? That I didn't know. Glenda Sue didn't have any money or jewels or stocks and bonds. She'd been as poor the day she died as she'd been the day she was born. There was the land, all twenty-two acres of it. Overworked farmland that wouldn't even grow thistles anymore. Although a hell of a lot of Oklahoma had oil under it, our little corner had always been presumed to be bone dry. And even so, nobody nowadays killed for oil. Not with the price per barrel as low as it was.

So why? I used the phone in the bedroom to call the office and tell 'em about the vandalism, then went on home to tell Melissa.

I wake up in Glenda Sue's bed, in Glenda Sue's trailer. My head feels like a watermelon after somebody's stomped it. I sit up gingerly swinging my legs to the floor. I'm naked. "Shit," I think. "What'd I do now?"

I pull my blue jeans that lay on the floor over to me with one foot and carefully put them on. Finding my T-shirt, I put that on too. I have no idea where my shirt is. I'm pretty sure I'd been wearing one. I can smell coffee and bacon frying and walk carefully out of the little master bedroom and down the short hall to the main room of the trailer.

Glenda Sue's standing at the stove, oven mitt on one hand, fork in the other. Hearing me, she glances in my direction. Her look isn't a friendly one.

"You sick?" she asks.

"I've felt better," I confess.

"Well, go outside if you're gonna throw up. I don't want the stench in the trailer."

"That's okay. I don't throw up."

She nods her head. "Yeah, that's right. I forgot."

She plays with the bacon some, then looks at me again. "You want eggs?"

I shrug. "Sure, why not?"

I feel better after I've finished eating. I sit at her little Formica-topped table while she cleans the dishes. After a few minutes, she comes to the table and sits, a coffee cup in her hand. She takes a sip, then looks at me.

"It's been five months since I've seen you. Then you show up here drunk as a skunk and wanna get laid."

"Glenda Sue . . ."

"In case nobody ever told you, you're not very good at it when you're drunk."

"I'm sorry..."

"You ever show up here again drunk, I'll take a baseball bat to you. Don't think I won't, just ask your old buddy Linn."

"Glenda Sue..."

"You wanna see me regular, fine. I wanna see you. Sober. We'll sleep together when we both feel up to it. We'll be a couple. We won't be me waiting here for you to come over every month or so to get some nooky. You understand?"

I nod my head.

"That's the only way it's gonna be," she says.

Again I nod my head.

"Okay, then, you wanna go back to bed?"

I nod my head and resist the urge to say, "Yes, ma'am."

There are still five cars in our turnaround at the house. One I recognized as Bert and Mavis Davis's, one Harmon Monk's big ol' Cadillac. The other two were my '55, and Jewel's wagon. The fifth, a white-on-white Lincoln Towncar, I didn't recognize.

I drove my squad car up and parked, trying not to block anybody, then walked on in the house. Jewel and her kids and Harmon, and Bert and Mavis and Kathy Ann, were all in the living room, coffee cups in hand and dessert plates balanced on their laps. Cups and plates littered every surface in the room. I've noticed since Harmon had entered Jewel's life again, she'd relaxed a lot in her mania about a clean house, but even so, this was stretching things a bit.

"Hey," I greeted, and everybody greeted me back. "Where's Melissa and Rebecca?"

Everybody looked from one to another, then Jewel Anne got to her feet and came over to me. Pointing out towards the back of the house, she said, "Outside. With a visitor."

Jewel liked to play her little games. "I noticed the Lincoln. Who is it?"

"Linn Robinson."

I went out the back door, passing Rebecca coming in. I ruffled her kinky hair and got a smile for my trouble, then kept on walking towards where I could see Melissa standing out back in the tall grass, beyond the place where I mowed, talking with a man. As I neared, I recognized him. Linn Robinson it was.

Standing back a ways, too far for him to comfortably shake my hand, I said, "Hey, Linn."

He looked up, a tight smile on his lips, and nodded his head curtly. "Milt. How're you?"

"Stupid question under the circumstances," I said.

"She's in God's lovin' arms now, Milt. Rest assured."

Melissa had turned to me and taken a few steps in my direction. Without thinking much about it, I slipped my arm across her shoulders. "What're you doing here, Linn?"

"Heard about Glenda Sue. Ardmore po-lice came by asking me about an alibi. I didn't have nothing to do with this here and you know it. But I thought I'd come down and pay my respects. Missed the funeral by a few minutes though. Then I found out Melissa was staying here with y'all, thought I'd come by."

"You through?"

"Milt, that's no way to behave," he said.

"Melissa, you got any more to say to this man?" I asked her, still looking hard at my old best friend.

"Not a goddamn thing," Melissa said, her voice soft.

But old Linn heard. "Girl, you watch your mouth. Don't go blaspheming the Lord. You got enough to pay for in the hereafter lest you be doing that."

With this parting bit of bullshit wisdom, he was gone.

"You did it?" I ask, trying to be cool.

"'Course," Linn answers, strapping up his shoulder pads.

"With Glenda Sue?"

He hits me on the shoulder and laughs. "Who else?"

"Well?"

"Well, what?"

"Well, you know..."

He grins. "Man, it was great! Hunnerd times better than playing a solo tune on the bone-a-phone. Know what I mean?"

I grin back. "Yeah, choking the chicken..."

"Wrestling the one-eyed cobra..."

"Flonging the dong..."

"Fuckin' ol' Rosey Palm..."

Later that evening I sat in my favorite chair in the living room, staring out the front windows at the partial hole in the ground that would someday be a pool, when little Rebecca crawled up in my lap.

"Well, hey, there," I said, putting my arm around her tiny back. "What brings you to visit?"

"Can I ask you a question?" she said.

"Certainly."

"What's a nigger?"

The hair on the back of my neck stood up, and my palms got clammy. "Where'd you hear that, honey?" I asked.

She rested her head against my shoulder. "That man, my grandpa. He told Mommy I was one. Am I?"

"No, you're not," I said. "And another thing, that man he may be your mommy's father, but he's not your grandpa. I am."

The little head popped up and she looked at me, her black eyes big as saucers. "You are?"

"I sure am."

"The best grandpa you'll ever have, too," Melissa said from the doorway.

Rebecca and I both looked. Rebecca's little hand went to her waist, an unconscious imitation of her mother's stance in the doorway.

"You didn't tell me he was my grandpa," she scolded.

"I forgot."

"How could you forget *that?*"

Melissa walked up to where her child and I sat in my chair and nuzzled her daughter's neck. "You get old like me, pumpkin, you forget things. It's a curse."

Rebecca put her arms around my neck and hugged. "Well, I won't forget," she said.

"Me neither," I replied.

FIVE

I SPENT TUESDAY MORNING working at Glenda Sue's trailer trying to see what I could see, which wasn't much, and the afternoon working a wreck out on Highway 5. No fatalities, thank God. I didn't think I could take looking at any more dead bodies for a while. Even ones I didn't know and love.

I got back to the station around 5 P.M., and found Kenneth Marshallton waiting for me. Kenneth was the assistant county attorney for Prophesy County. He was about thirty-four, thirty-five years old, married to the daughter of a former governor, and figured he'd be sleeping in his father-in-law's former bed real soon. He was dressed in a neat three-piece suit, dark blue pinstripe, and his shoes were shined. Hardly could tell he went to OU on scholarship 'cause his farmer daddy couldn't afford to send him.

"Kenneth," I said, slipping into my own office and sitting in my own visitor's chair, since his royal high-ass was sitting in mine behind the desk.

He swiveled around a few times, looking out my windows. Then turned back to me. "Kovak."

We nodded.

"I understand you were personally acquainted with the deceased," he said, looking at his papers. "Glenda Sue Robinson."

"That's right."

"You want to tell me about your relationship?"

Not all that goddamned much I didn't. No. "We were dating," I answered.

"Dating." He said it like it sounded funny to him. Absolutely hysterical.

"Yeah, that's right," I said, my temper beginning to flare. "Dating."

"You sleep with her?"

"No. But we had sex on a regular basis."

His face got a tight look I enjoyed a lot. He pursed his lips in and out a few times, then said, "Why don't you save the smart-ass, Kovak? This isn't the place for it."

"No, sir, it isn't. This is the place where I do my work. This is my office. Now if you got something to say to me, questions you want to ask, you just go ahead. But it's quitting time for me, so I'd like to make it quick."

"We'll take just as much time as I think necessary, Deputy," he said, leaning back in my chair. I didn't have the heart to tell him the back of my swivel was a little bit on the blink. The back panel sprung and fell, and he swept his hand out, resting it against the wall to keep from falling over.

I'm ashamed of myself, but I laughed. Right out loud. Kenneth Marshallton stood up and came around the desk, leaning one hip against the side. "You're the last one saw the woman alive, Kovak. By your own admission, you had a fight with her. Now... you want to tell me what *really* happened that night?"

"I think I already told you that, Kenny," Elberry Blankenship said from the doorway. Marshallton frowned at the "Kenny" but let it go.

"I'd like to hear it from him, Sheriff, if you don't mind."

"Well, I do mind. We'll be real happy to cooperate with you, Kenny. But Milt's got work to do. He already told me he didn't see nothing or nobody hanging around the trailer that night. That's all you need to know."

"Look, Sheriff..."

Elberry went up to Marshallton and clapped him on the back, one hand pulling him up and out the door. "You got any more questions, Kenny, you come on back anytime, you hear?" In two minutes, Kenneth Marshallton was out of the building.

If Marshallton was anything, it was a politician, and he knew messing with the sheriff wasn't the political thing to do. Elberry Blankenship on your side come election time in Prophesy County was a good thing. Elberry Blankenship against you come election time, you might as well stay home.

The sheriff came back and stood at the door of my office, watching me as I got my stuff ready to go. "You okay?" he asked.

"Now that you got rid of the snot-nosed brat, yeah."

"He's harmless."

I walked to the door and shook his hand. "Thanks just the same."

"You go on home now, Milt. See you in the morning."

The next day, Wednesday, Melissa rode into town with me, and I dropped her off at Long-branch Memorial Hospital where she was going for a job interview. I found out Melissa was a social worker by trade, with a Masters degree. Impressive, I thought. The job was working for the staff psychiatrist, a new position they put in at the hospital, not to be confused with the psychologist who ran the outpatient counseling service, Dr. Marston, who Jewel and I saw on a semiregular basis. I wished Melissa luck and dropped her off, promising to pick her up at lunchtime and truck her back to the mountain.

I spent that morning looking over wanted posters from the FBI and the Oklahoma State Police, looking for likely suspects. They all seemed likely to me. At lunch I picked up Melissa and took her to eat at Bernie's Chat and Chew, not wanting to patronize the Longbranch Inn just yet. Maybe never. I couldn't rightly see walking into the place and sitting down at a table and not having Glenda Sue come up to serve me. Being served by some other waitress seemed like a sort of betrayal, I guess.

"Well, hell, it must be Wednesday," Loretta Dubchek says as I walk in the door of the Long-branch Inn.

"Hey, Loretta," I say, sauntering over to my usual table. Glenda Sue comes out of the kitchen with a quart jar of iced tea and sets it down in front of me.

"Chicken-fried steak be ready in a minute, hon," she says.

"Time to sit and chat?"

"Always."

"So how'd the interview go?" I asked Melissa over our liver and onion daily special.

"Pretty good. Dr. McDonnell is quite impressive. She's . . ."

"She?"

Melissa gave me one of them looks women give men when they say something stupid. "Yes, she, Milt. They allow women to become doctors now, did you hear?"

"Don't get smart."

"Anyway, she was an undergrad at Harvard and got her medical training at Johns Hopkins. What she wants is someone to take family histories of the patients she'll be seeing and do some counseling with the families. And the money's not bad."

"Well, I'm glad you decided to stay on here. And I want you to know, Jewel and I discussed it and you can stay with us as long as you need."

Melissa put her hand on mine across the table and smiled. "Thanks, Milt. You know, you and Jewel are more family than I've had in a long time."

I patted her hand with my other hand and cleared my throat. "Well, anyway, you about through?"

Melissa leaned back in her chair and laughed at me, which is something women do when men can't handle sentimental stuff. They think that's funny. Women, as a general rule, and I'm not being sexist here or anything, have strange senses of humor.

"What are you laughing at, girl?" I said, slurping iced tea as a kind of shield.

"You. You get embarrassed so easily."

"No, I don't."

"Yes, you do. And now I'm going to say something that should put you in a coma."

"Gee whiz, kid, thanks bunches."

Again Melissa laughed. "You've always been my hero," she said, smiling at me.

"You 'bout through with that dinner?"

"Listen to me." Her hand came out again and grasped mine. "When I was a little girl, you were the white knight that came to Mama's rescue...."

"It wasn't just me. All the deputies came out one time or another...."

"Yeah, but to them it was just a job. To you it was personal. Even little as I was, I knew that. I wasn't the least bit surprised that you and Mama were seeing each other. It seemed right. When I was little, I used to pretend you were my daddy...."

"Melissa..."

She laughed at my discomposure. "Well, it's true! And now you're my baby's grandpa. A dream come true."

I wiped my mouth with my napkin and stood up. "Best be heading back to the house," I said, and I woulda shuffled my toe in the dirt if Bernie's Chat and Chew hadn't just been recently swept.

"Linn, goddamn it!" I grab at his shirt, ripping it, pulling him off Glenda Sue. Her arms hang at a weird angle to her body.

Sonny Lee, the other deputy, takes Linn, and I bend down over Glenda Sue. "Looks bad," I say.

"Broken," she says.

I go out to the squad car and call an ambulance.

"Goddamn bitch!" Linn shouts as Sonny Lee pushed his head down getting him in the backseat.

"You're pressing charges this time, Glenny," I say, sitting with her waiting for the ambulance, as Sonny Lee drives off in the squad car with Linn.

"Why?" Glenda Sue asked, holding her arm with the other hand. "How long can you keep him? A day? Two? He'll just be back and madder than ever. What good would it do?"

"Glenny..."

"Don't call me that."

I sigh and sit down on the floor next to her. Melissa crawls between us, on her mama's good side, and puts her head in her mama's lap. And we wait.

We headed out to the car and on towards my mountain, where Jewel was keeping Rebecca. She had already offered to serve as baby-sitter when Melissa got a job. Not that it was any big sacrifice on Jewel's part. I think she liked to play more than the kid did.

I didn't notice anything wrong when I pulled into the drive and up to the house. It was quiet, but how much noise could one little kid and a grown-up make? We parked the car and headed to the front door. I had been planning on just dropping Melissa off and heading back for town, but remembered I needed some papers I'd left in my room. I still didn't notice anything wrong when I opened the front door. Except it was quiet. But kids take naps. And so do grown-ups sometimes.

"Jewel Anne?" I called out, but there was no answer. That's when I glanced from the foyer into the living room. The place had been demolished. Sofa cushions ripped open, logs and ash pulled out of the fireplace, tables broken.

I backed up into Melissa, pushing her towards the front door. "Go outside," I said softly.

She tried to move around me, to see what I'd seen. I turned and grabbed her by the shoulders. "Get outside and use my radio to call in. Tell 'em who you are and where you are, and tell 'em to send a squad car immediately."

"Rebecca!" Melissa said, trying to get around me again.

I shoved her out the door. "Do what I say!" I shouted, watching for a second until I knew that she would. That's when I thought to pull my pistol out. I keep it in a holster on my right hip and most times forget it's there. I looked into the dining room, seeing my mama's broken china scattered all around the room. I opened the French doors between the dining room and the little room where Melissa and Rebecca stayed. It was empty, but all their belongings had been torn and broken.

I backtracked into the foyer and went straight ahead to the kitchen. The place was a mess, food from the refrigerator dumped on the floor, kitchen cabinets opened and all the contents thrown and broken on the floor. And written in something red, something I hoped to hell was ketchup, on the wall next to the door to the utility room, were the words, "nigger-lover."

Leaning up against the wall, my gun barrel held skyward, I inched my way to the door to the utility room, which was slightly ajar. Using my left leg, I pivoted and kicked the door open, swinging my body around and gripping the gun with both hands. But the utility room was empty.

I walked gingerly through the mess in the kitchen, heading for the door to the master bedroom, Jewel's bedroom, on the far side of the kitchen.

That's when I heard Melissa, at the front door, calling me. "Milt?"

"Stay out!" I ordered. "Get in the car and lock the doors!"

When I heard her scurry away, I moved on to the bedroom door, repeating my performance at the utility room. I stood there looking at the devastation of my sister's room for a full minute before I noticed that one of the bundles of clothes had arms and legs sticking out of it. I holstered my gun and ran into the room.

Jewel lay in a heap on her stomach on the bedroom floor, bad leg bunched under her at a weird angle, hands tied behind her, mouth taped with duct tape. Her eyes were closed. When I ripped the tape from her mouth, the eyes opened and she screamed.

"Shit, Milton!"

Things were indeed bad. Jewel Anne never cussed.

"What happened?" I asked, untying her hands.

"Rebecca! Where's Rebecca?"

"She's not in here?"

Jewel shook her head, grimacing with pain. I helped her to her feet, but she almost fell due to the new injury to the bad leg. I sat her down on what was left of her bed and began to rub her leg, trying to get the circulation going again. She winced in pain but didn't cry out.

"Three men burst in here. All wearing ski masks. Rebecca and I were in the kitchen, fixing lunch..."

"Fixing lunch? It's only a little after one now. When was that?"

Jewel shook her head. "About...eleven thirty, I think."

"Then what happened?"

Again, she shook her head. "I don't know... they... grabbed me... Rebecca screamed... Oh, God, Milt, where's Rebecca?"

That, indeed, was the $64,000 question. From the foyer, I again heard Melissa. "Milt! The sheriff car's here! Where's Rebecca?"

I noticed a tinge of panic in Melissa's voice. I didn't answer. I figured there'd be more than a tinge in mine if I did. I went to the front of the house and met Elberry Blankenship as he got out of his car. Following close behind were Mike Neils and Dalton Pettigrew.

"What the hell's going on?" the sheriff demanded.

Briefly, I told him. Melissa must have moved closer, because she heard, then screamed and ran for the house. With damn near the entire sheriff's department fast on her heels.

Jewel Anne was already up and moving through the rooms, tears streaming down her face and calling, "Rebecca! Rebecca!" over and over.

We searched the house from stem to stern, including the attic crawl space, with nothing to show for our efforts, except cobwebs in our hair. Jewel had uprighted a chair in the living room and had set Melissa down in it, holding her while she sobbed.

"Let's move the search outside," the sheriff said. "We'll do a quick prelim on your property, then call in reinforcements to search the woods."

"The storm cellar!" Jewel said.

I looked at her. "Jesus Christ!"

I ran out the back door and to the doors leading to the storm cellar. A stick was stuck between the handles of the door. A stick I never put there. I pulled it out quickly and grabbed the flashlight off Mike Neils's Sam Browne belt. I opened the doors wide and flashed the light. That's when I heard the whimper. I forced myself to move the light slowly until I found her, huddled in a corner, her face wet from tears, but not a mark on her.

"Hush, baby," I cooed. "Grandpa's here."

I walked down the ladder and picked her up and cuddled her in my arms. It had never felt so good before to hold a little kid. Never. Above me, I heard Dalton call out, "We found her!" And in a minute Melissa was stumbling down the ladder.

Elberry called his wife, Nadine, and in less than twenty minutes, Jewel, Melissa, and Rebecca were being whisked away to the Blankenship home. Jewel would call the school from there and tell the principal to have her children wait to be picked up. Not to take the bus home. It might be a while before anybody except me went back into that house.

Now that everybody was safe and sound, I took a good look at the devastation of my home. Jewel's baby grand piano had its own room, the sun room attached to the back of the living room. It had had an ax taken to it and lay in a splintered heap on the hardwood floors. The mattress of every bed in the house had been ripped to shreds, the tops and bottoms. Even boxes in the attic crawl space had been broken into, their contents slashed or broken and heaped on the floor.

There didn't appear to be one salvageable thing in the entire house. Nothing me, my sister, or the kids owned had been spared. Clothes had been slashed to ribbons. Blow dryers had been thrown to the floor and then apparently smashed with a heavy foot. Marlene's makeup case had been tossed and stepped in, Pretty-as-a-Pinkture-colored footsteps stained the upstairs carpet. Records broken, tapes torn, books slashed. The door to my little refrigerator had been pulled off its hinges, and the beer inside had been opened, its contents poured over my belongings.

The sheriff sent Mike and Dalton back to the office, and he and I sat down on the front porch steps.

"Something's going on, Sheriff," I said.

"No shit."

"I mean, Glenda Sue's murder wasn't just some random nut case. Somebody went by her place looking for something. They tortured her to find out where it was. They didn't reckon with the fact that after living with Linn Robinson for all those years, Glenda Sue had a real high pain threshold. After they killed her, they came back, ransacked her place, and then came over here. I'm not sure if they came here because of me or because of Melissa. But they came here looking for whatever it is they think Glenda Sue had. And one thing I'd really like to know is where the hell them two—Kretcher and Bass—were during all this."

"Well, I don't know about them. Nobody's seen hide nor hair of them since they jumped bail. Seems stupid to me that they'd be hanging around here now. But the other, somebody looking for something, that seems likely," the sheriff agreed, nodding his head. "But what the hell did Glenda Sue have they could want?"

"You got me by the ass."

"Okay," he said, "let's assume she had something. They wanted it. We can assume they didn't find it when they kilt her 'cause they went back to her place again looking for it. We can assume they didn't find it at her place, 'cause they came here looking for it. You think you had it?"

"How the hell do I know?"

"She leave anything with you?"

"No. Not ever."

"Where else would she put something?"

I shrugged. "Her car?"

The sheriff shook his head. "Naw. They took that apart when they took apart her trailer."

"Oh. I didn't see that."

"Naw. We found it after you left the scene. I didn't feel it worth mentioning to you at the time."

"She had a locker at the Longbranch. All the waitresses got lockers."

"Well, then, let's go."

We hopped in the sheriff's car and hightailed it back to Longbranch. With a slight detour.

"Sheriff, you mind stopping at the Quick Mart?" I asked.

He agreed and pulled in. I got out, went to the counter, and bought a pack of Marlboro and a cheap lighter. I lit up on my way to the car and almost passed out. But I'm nothing if not stubborn. I puffed my way back to the car.

"What the hell do you think you're doing?" the sheriff demanded.

"Smoking a cigarette."

"You don't smoke."

"I do now."

"There's a county ordinance says no smoking in county vehicles, or don't you read the newsletter?"

I wasn't about to admit that, no, I didn't read the damn newsletters ever if I could help it, so I dropped the cigarette out the open door of the car and squashed it with the heel of my shoe, then sat back and watched the world spin as the sheriff drove on to the Longbranch Inn.

"Hey, Glen, throw it!" I yell.

"Throw it to me, Glen!" Linn yells.

"Shut up or I ain't throwing it to nobody!" Glenda Sue calls back, running long, the football tucked under her arm, her short blonde hair wet with sweat.

I run after her, tackling her and knocking her to the ground.

"You shithead!" she yells.

"You were supposed to throw it," I say, lying on top of her. She pushes out from under me, rolls me over, and sits down on top of me. Her top two buttons have come undone, and I can see inside her blouse.

I scurry out from under her, my face turning red.

"What's wrong with you?" Glenda Sue demands.

"Nothing," I say, standing up. "I gotta go home. Dinnertime."

I leave Linn and Glenda Sue standing there staring after me. Everything has suddenly changed. I have to tell Linn. Glenda Sue has grown boobs.

Once there, we went into Maynard Dabney's little office.

"Hey, Maynard," the sheriff said, sticking out his hand.

Dabney shook hands with both of us. "What can I do for you, Elberry? You get a chance yet to get out to the deer lease?"

"Yeah, made it out there last weekend, but I didn't bag nothing. Saw me a beaut though. Eight-point buck. Too far away. I wanna thank you again for letting me use that lease. Best one around here, I swear to God."

"My pleasure," Dabney said. "Maybe you'll put a good word in for me with the health inspector next time he comes around." Everybody laughed. Even me. You gotta be polite.

The sheriff cleared his throat. "We need to see Glenda Sue's locker. We don't have a court order, but we could get one."

"Oh, now, Elberry, don't be like that! I wanna cooperate. Glenda Sue was a good woman. I wanna know who done this much as you. Only thing is, we got us a new waitress to take her place, and I done give her Glenda Sue's locker."

"What'd you do with Glenda Sue's stuff?" I asked.

"Well, wasn't much. Some hair spray and a sweater, and an extra pair of shoes. And some stockings is all. I give 'em to Loretta. Just a minute."

Dabney went to the door of his office and called "Loretta!" and then came and sat back down.

Loretta Dubchek came to the door. She was married to Leon Dubchek had the Firestone outlet on Sandy Road. She'd worked with Glenda Sue longer than any of the other waitresses, been at the Longbranch almost twenty-five years. She was a big woman in her late forties, dyed black hair and lipstick redder than fresh blood.

"Yeah, Maynard? Oh, hi, Milt, Sheriff. Milt, I sure am sorry..."

"You know that stuffa Glenda Sue's I give you?" Dabney interrupted. "What'd you do with it?"

"Oh, I got it in a box in the back of my car. I was gonna bring it by your place, Milt, for that girl of her'n. Figure she might want what was her mama's."

I stood up. "That's mighty nice of you, Loretta. Mind if I take a look?"

Loretta fished in the pocket of her apron and brought out a set of keys. "This here one's for the trunk. It's the black LTD out back."

We thanked her and headed out to the back parking lot of the Longbranch Inn, finding the ten-year-old LTD without much trouble. The key worked fine, and the trunk lid opened. And there was the box. Besides what Maynard Dabney had said, there was a birthday card from me for her birthday three weeks back, plus the little glass bud vase, one of them ones with two stems that twist around each other, that I'd given her for her birthday with two long-stemmed roses. Made me kinda heartsick just to look at it. There was also a menu from a new pizza service that delivered. But there was nothing that would interest anybody enough to kill for, I figured.

"I'd still like to have me a look-see at that locker," I told the sheriff.

He nodded and we marched back in the office. Maynard Dabney called his new waitress in, who I recognized as Bobbie Lynn Schafner. I knew the Schafner family from church, the mama and daddy and all seven younger Schafners. Bobbie Lynn was the eldest at eighteen. Each of the Schafner children was named Lynn. Like Bobbie Lynn, Jessie Lynn, Annie Lynn, and a bunch of other Lynns.

They were a nice family, if a touch unimaginative. Dabney explained the situation, and Bobbie Lynn gladly took us to her locker and unlocked it.

There was nothing in it but a sweater, a pair of high heels, and a makeup kit.

"If you wouldn't mind too much, Miz Bobbie Lynn," the sheriff said, "would you just take all this stuff out so we can see it emptylike?"

"Sure, Sheriff," the girl said, her face plainly saying she thought the both of us a bit strange.

Bobbie Lynn took her stuff and put it on a table and went back to work, while the sheriff and I stood and stared at the empty locker. Empty except for a mirror on the back. I looked at the mirror for a minute, remembering one Jewel Anne had bought for Marlene's school locker at the beginning of the school year. It had little magnets on the back. I wondered if this was the same kind. I reached out my hand and tugged at the mirror, and sure enough, it came off in my hand. When it did, something fell from behind it.

The sheriff reached down to the bottom of the locker and picked up the paper that had fallen. But it wasn't just a piece of paper. It was a paper envelope with the American Airlines logo on the front. Opening it, we found a one-way ticket to

Dallas-Fort Worth, with a connecting direct American flight to Paris, France, in the name of Glenda Sue Robinson. The date of both flights were the day after Glenda Sue was murdered.

SIX

I WAS WALKING in this big empty building over cobblestones. The only sound the echoing of my shoes. None of it was familiar, even though I knew it was. I walked until I came to an escalator going up. I stepped on to silence so complete it was like watching a TV screen with the sound off.

As I reached the middle of the trip up, I saw the child at the top. Except this time it wasn't some unknown little boy with motel-room-art eyes. It was Rebecca. And then came the woman legs. The twisted, braced woman legs. And the hand. And the terror. And my scream.

Only this time when I woke up, I wasn't alone. Three pairs of angry eyes stared back at me. Leonard's, Carl's, and the sheriff's.

"What the hell's wrong with you?" the sheriff demanded, looking no less the authority figure in his white pajamas with the little red and blue sailboats and yellow anchors.

I apologized and reached for a cigarette. "If you're gonna do that," the sheriff said, "go outside. Nadine'll nail my hide to the wall, she catches anybody smoking in this house."

I got up and went outside and sat in a metal lawn chair, trying to ignore the chilly night air. Used to be, when I smoked twenty years ago, you could light up anywhere. People on TV used to have little silver cigarette boxes on their coffee tables and would offer one to the mailman even. So far that day, I'd been kicked out of a car and a house and made to sit by the kitchen at a restaurant just because I wanted to smoke a cigarette. Sometimes the unfairness of life really gets me down.

'Course, dwelling on the inhumanities smokers put up with kept me from dwelling on the god-awful dream. I was beginning to think maybe I might want to schedule an appointment with Mr. Marston all for myself. Talk about this. Find out why. Find a way to make it go away.

After getting back to the station earlier that day, I'd called American Airlines and confirmed the tickets. Reservations for a flight to Paris, France, with connecting flight in Dallas from Tulsa had been made four days in advance. The first-class ticket had been mailed to Glenda Sue's home address. No one, of course, had used the ticket.

And Friday night she hadn't wanted to marry me. Maybe thinking I'd cramp her style in Paris. Paris! Jesus. Glenda Sue in Paris. And where in the hell had she gotten the money for a ticket to Paris? Even the one-way ticket had to cost over a thousand bucks. Specially if she was going first-class. Glenda Sue had been skipping town in style. And somebody had killed her. And somebody was looking for something. It didn't take a whole lot of smarts to put two and two together and come up with the fact that a sizable amount of cash was involved. But I didn't want to think about that. About Glenda Sue skipping out on me. 'Cause that's what it meant. Glenda Sue had been about to leave me. Which put me back in mind as everybody's prime suspect. Even mine. Maybe I'd found out about her leaving me, killed her in a rage, then got amnesia? Shit.

"Well, I ain't staying around here after I graduate," Glenda Sue says.

"Ha. Where you think you're going?" Linn asks.

Glenda Sue spits into a cup. The three of us sit in a circle on the fifty yard line of the football field, chewing tobacco and spitting into a paper cup.

"I'm gonna be a stewardess, for Pan Am or something like that, so I can travel all over the world. See things. Like the Great Wall of China and the Eiffel Tower and London Bridge..."

"Shit," Linn says. *"You'll never be a stewardess."*

"Why not?" Glenda Sue asks and spits.

Linn and I both look at her fourteen-year-old breasts. They're bigger than my mama's, the only way I know how to judge breasts.

"Your titties is too big," Linn says, spitting into the cup from several feet away, missing and hitting my high-top.

"Shit!" I say, wiping the spittle off on the grass. "Watch it!"

"Yeah, sorry."

Glenda Sue looks down at her chest. "What's wrong with my titties?"

"Nothing," Linn says, grinning slyly. "I like your titties personally, but you ever seen pictures of them stewardesses? They're all real skinny. And tall."

"Well, maybe I won't be a stewardess then, but I'm sure as hell not staying around this dump."

"Yeah, I bet," Linn says.

Then, of course, I had to think about my house, my beautiful house that had been ravaged twice in little more than a month. First the tornado, then the vandalism. When I'd called Lucille Bright, my insurance agent, she hadn't been really happy with two claims so close together. Said the insurance carrier was gonna want to look into it. Which meant they were gonna try to come up with a way of not paying. But the mood I was in, I thought just let 'em. I'd sue their asses off. I been paying my premiums once a month like clockwork since I bought the house.

All the furniture, except for my bedroom suite and my chair in the living room, belonged to Jewel Anne, and she kept a separate policy on that. One that had been taxed with the tornado due to all Leonard's belongings in the garage apartment being blown to Kansas. But her insurance agent was her ex-next door neighbor from Houston, and we both knew she'd have no trouble collecting. Chuck Lancaster would just as soon snap the neck of any old insurance adjuster who wanted to deny Jewel Anne a claim.

But still and all, it would be a while before we could get back to living in the house. It would need new carpet where there had been carpet, the hardwoods would have to be refinished, and most of the walls repainted and repapered.

And then there would be the replacing. Replacing furniture, appliances, TVs, stereos, dishes, pictures, books, records, clothes, and a million other things that people need to have a happy life. Like food processors and woks and Water Piks and curling irons. Just thinking about it made my mind reel.

When I moved into my house on Mountain Falls Road, everything I owned fit in the trunk of my '55, except for the bedroom set and the chair. I had four plates, four bowls, four cups, two glasses, a knife, fork, and spoon, and a frying pan. I was jim-dandy at fixing soup in a frying pan. Now, after less than a year of Jewel living with me, I would actually miss the food processor and Water Pik and pictures and books and records, etc., etc., etc. I had no personal need for the curling iron though. But you can sure get attached to stuff. You really can. Like the picture I had that hung over the mantle that had been given to me by a former lady friend. Now slashed to ribbons. The last reminder of a love affair gone bad. I'd miss that picture and the stabbing pain I got every time I looked at it.

But everybody was okay, there was that. I thought for a while about what Jewel and Rebecca had been able to tell us. Three men in ski masks. They'd been white, Jewel had said, she could tell by their hands. One was tallish, one was shortish, and one was mediumish. One had a gruff voice and the other two didn't speak. She couldn't remember if it was the tallish, shortish or mediumish one who spoke. They all three wore jeans and work boots, and two wore regular shirts and one wore a T-shirt with a Coors logo.

Rebecca said that the man who had taken her had carried her to the doors to the storm cellar and, after opening them, had ordered her to walk down the ladder. She'd been scared. That's all she remembered. Jewel had a knot on her head where she'd either been hit or had fallen, she couldn't remember which. Evinrude, my orange tabby cat, had disappeared during the fracas. I figured when he reappeared, he wouldn't be able to tell me much more. And that's all we had. Which sure as hell wasn't much.

I snuffed out my cigarette and went back into the house, into the spare room where us guys were camped, and crawled back into my sleeping bag, trying for a dreamless sleep.

"Bet you a buck you won't do it," Linn jeers at me.

"I don't see no reason why I should do it. It's stupid."

"You're just a chicken shit."

"Stealin's stealin', way I look at it."

Linn starts making clucking noises, imitating a chicken.

"Shit, Linn, leave him alone," Glenda Sue says.

"Butt out, girl. Nobody's talking to you."

"You want somebody to steal that damn knife, I'll do it!"

"Glenny..." I call, but she's on her way into the T G & Y. Linn and I stand outside, not looking at each other. In about ten minutes, Glenda Sue comes out and thrusts the pocket knife in Linn's hand.

"Here, don't say come Christmas you ain't got your present from me, asshole!"

Glenda Sue takes my arm and we walk off away from town. In my ear, she whispers. "You owe me half a buck seventy-five."

I laugh. "You paid for it?"

"Of course, what you think, I'm stupid? You tell Linn though, I'll chop off your head and tell God you died."

The next morning I woke up to the smell of frying bacon. God, how I loved that smell. My sister Jewel is not the best cook in the world. In fact, I believe she's in the finals for the worst cook in the world contest. There are three things that smell better than sin: bacon frying, onions frying, and coffee perking. Jewel's the only person I ever heard of who could do those things and get no smell. But that morning I woke up in Nadine Blankenship's house, and Nadine Blankenship sure knew how to make frying bacon smell.

I got dressed and helped the sheriff pull the picnic table into the kitchen from the backyard, setting it up next to the kitchen table so there'd be enough room for all the extra people. Then I sipped the best coffee in the world while I watched the womenfolk set the table. Mrs. Blankenship fixed enough food to feed an army, which is just about how many people we had. Well, enough for a small

Central American army maybe. We had bacon, sausage and ham, eggs, hashbrowns, biscuits, and coffee. I ate until I thought I'd die of sheer pleasure.

Then the sheriff and I left the womenfolk and children to do whatever it is they do, and went on to the station. I spent the morning on paperwork and the afternoon talking to a group at the high school on the horrors of drugs. My nephew Leonard was part of the group, and he had a great time making faces at me and trying to get me to laugh while I was giving my speech. It didn't work. After all, I'm the head deputy of the Prophesy County Sheriff's Department. I got way too much class for that.

When I got back to the station, there was a message to call Jewel. I dialed the sheriff's home number.

"Hey, Miz Blankenship," I said when she answered the phone, "this is Milt. Jewel there?"

"No, Milt, she's over at the Longbranch. Call her there and she'll explain." The sheriff's wife gave me a number, and I thanked her, hung up, and dialed.

Jewel answered on the first ring. "Where are you?" I asked.

"Sitting in my room," she replied.

"What room?"

"One of the rooms my insurance company is paying for for an indefinite period."

"No shit? How indefinite?"

"Long as it takes to fix the house. We have four rooms. Marlene and I will share one, the boys'll share another, Melissa and Rebecca in the third, and you all by your lonesome."

"Poor me," I said smiling, considering the one night I'd spent in the company of my two nephews and the sheriff, one night too many. "Did they give you any trouble about Melissa and Rebecca?"

"No. Chuck said since they had belongings in the house that were also destroyed and that they'd been there for more than a month . . ."

"Jewel, they've only been there . . ."

"For more than a month, that makes them residents, and they get a room, too."

I could hear Chuck talking my sister into this one. Jewel Anne never has been much on stretching truths. Mama told her it wasn't ladylike.

"What's my room number?" I asked.

"Four-twelve. I'm in four-eleven across the hall. Come by here and I'll give you the key."

"Be there about five," I said and rang off.

I hadn't been in the hotel side of the Longbranch Inn in about ten years. The restaurant had its own separate entrance, so there was no need to go into the hotel. I knew there'd been some remodeling done five years back when Maynard Dabney'd bought the place. But I was still surprised by the foyer. Used to be it was a barren, dark place smelling like dust and mildew, but the remodeling had done wonders.

One wall had been torn down and glass put in, giving the place some light. The old hardwood floors had been covered with an industrial carpet with a bright floral design in beige and dark green, with sprigs of orangy-red. Maynard had brought in some of those round seats you used to see in old hotels, the ones with the back a cylinder going up the middle and usually tufted in red velvet. The seats were done in a dark green velvet, like the green in the carpet, and they looked real nice. New light fixtures of brass hung on the walls next to paintings of English-type hunting scenes. All in all, it was a real pretty place. And it smelled good.

I went up to the desk, which was the same old one, but I didn't blame Maynard for not tearing that down. It had been the one distinguished thing about the old Longbranch. Long and carved of some good dark wood, it was ornate almost to the point of being silly, if it hadn't been so damn nice looking. And it went well with the new decor. The girl behind the desk was Jasmine Bodine's younger daughter, Marigold.

I said, "Hey, Marigold, how you doing?"

Marigold smiled sadly. Jasmine's maiden name had been Nail and all them Nail girls, Jasmine, Marigold, Lily, Rose, and Violet, were the saddest people I'd ever met. Strangely enough, their one brother, Dwight, was a real cheerful fella. "I'm fine," she said, her tone of voice denying the words. "How're you?"

"Just fine," I replied, smiling brightly. The Nail girls always had that effect on me. Made me want to smile, laugh, tell jokes, anything to cheer them up. "Jewel said she has my room key, so I'll just go on up," I said.

Marigold smiled sadly and nodded her head. I headed for the elevator and rode up to the fourth floor, then walked down the hall to room four-eleven and knocked on the door.

"Who is it?" came Marlene's voice.

"Your favorite uncle," I replied.

"Do I have one of those?" I heard my niece cheerfully ask her mama.

"Open the door," Jewel ordered from the other side.

Marlene opened the door grinning. "Oh, it's you!" she said.

"Funny as a truckload of dead armadillos," I replied poking her in the ribs and walking past her to where my sister sat at a little table and chair by the window that overlooked Henderson's Drugs and Sundries. She had pen and paper in hand and was making a list. Jewel Anne truly loved her lists. She was what you might call a list-making fool.

"Okay," she said, finishing her writing with a flourish, "you think the sheriff'll give you time off tomorrow?"

Never one to jump in blindly when it had anything to do with a list my sister made, I said, "Hard to tell. Can't rightly say. Whatja got there?"

I reached out my hand for the list, but she swatted it with hers and pulled the paper out of my reach. She never let me touch her lists anymore because of that one time I tore one up. Women are so goddamn sensitive.

"Things to do tomorrow," she read. "One. Go to house. Two. Sort what is to be thrown away, what is to be salvaged. Three. Put in two different stacks. Four. Throw away throwaways. Five. Clean one room to keep salvageables in. Six. Begin making lists of what is to be replaced. Seven . . ."

"Yeah, yeah," I said, sinking down on one of the two double beds in the room. "Sounds like great fun's to be had by all."

"Oh, gosh," she said, returning feverishly to her list. "I forgot to put 'pick up garbage bags.' Where should that go?"

"Where's my key?" I asked, standing up from the bed. Jewel pointed vaguely towards the dresser, where I saw a key. I went for it like a snake on a June bug, but got caught slipping out by my darling niece.

"Uncle Milt," she whispered, "tomorrow's a teacher's meeting day. No school. You can't leave us alone with Mama! She'll work us to death!"

"I know," I said and patted her on the head. "And you were so young and pretty."

"You're not very funny!" The look of anguish on Marlene's face made me feel almost sorry for her.

I sighed. "I'll call the sheriff. See what I can do about getting off." She smiled and I glared at her and left.

As I was unlocking the door to my room, the door next to it opened, and Melissa popped her head out. Seeing me, she smiled. "I hoped that was you I heard."

I smiled back. "Hey, there, kid, how's it going? Where's my grandbaby?"

The little curly head popped out of the room, and Rebecca ran into my arms. "Grandpa!" she said as I lifted her into my arms. She kissed me on the cheek, and I felt better than I had most of my life.

"What've you two been up to today?" I asked, carrying Rebecca towards the door to their room. Melissa opened it wider and I took Rebecca inside, bouncing her on the bed and listening to her giggle.

"Auntie Jewel took me to a toy store! See what I got?" She scrambled off the bed and headed to a corner of the room, where she began holding up assorted toys she'd acquired that day. "And this, and this, and this here . . ."

"You can show Grandpa that stuff later, honey. Right now you get in that tub. The water's getting cold." Melissa took the child into the bathroom to get her ready for her bath, while I sat on the bed and waited.

"You can play for fifteen minutes," Melissa said, coming out and shutting the door about halfway. "Then I'm going to call time, and that's when you wash. And you wash everything, you hear? Behind your ears, between your toes, under your eyeballs . . ."

Rebecca giggled and Melissa came over and sat on the bed next to me. "Guess what?" she said, her face all grins.

"Elvis was spotted at the American Legion Hall."

"No. At least I don't think so. But..." She stretched it out, grinning bigger than ever. "I got the job!"

I hugged her. "Honey, that's great! When do you start?"

"Monday. So I can help Jewel with the house tomorrow."

"Good, now I don't have to go."

Melissa hit me on the arm. "Yes, you do! We need a strong he-man type for heavy lifting and light hauling. We figure you can rent one."

"Girl, you got your mama's mouth on you."

Melissa shrugged. "I guess that's not all bad."

"Glenda Sue, you can't go on shooting at Linn like this," I say.

"Then tell the shithead to stay away from me and my kid! Milton, you hear what I'm saying?"

"I hear you, but one thing that girl of yours don't need is a dead daddy and a mama on death row."

"I tell you what, Milt, I promise I won't kill him, will that do?"

"You're gonna stop shooting at him?"

"Hell no, I just won't kill him."

"No, it's not all bad. Perturbing, aggravating, exasperating..." Again with the hit on the arm. "But not all bad," I finished up, standing. "I gotta go check out my room. Congratulations on the job." I went to the door of the bathroom and called, "Rebecca. I gotta go. See you at dinner, sweetheart."

"Okay, Grandpa." I grinned and left.

I went to my room and checked it out. It looked exactly like Melissa's room. Down to the bedspread and drapes. The only thing different was the packages of T-shirts, shorts, and socks and the razor and toothbrush on the bed. Brand-new. And a bottle of Aqua Velva. I preferred Old Spice, but my sister likes Aqua Velva, and it was her dime so what the hell. I figured I had her to thank for all this. Either her or the underwear fairy. I'd noticed back at the house, the vandals hadn't even left us our unmentionables.

I took a shower and changed into the fresh underwear, pulling the twice-worn wool pants to my suit back up and spraying the pits of my twice-worn shirt with Right Guard. I needed to get to the store. The only thing in life I hate more than clothes shopping is having a root canal. And I prefer the root canal if they give me laughing gas. I tend toward white oxford cloth shirts and black socks. That way no one knows if your socks are mismatched or you wore the same shirt the day before. But at least, before the vandalism, I had five of the damn white shirts and six or seven pairs of black socks. Jewel may have replaced the socks, but I really was wearing the same shirt as I had been the day before the day before.

By the time I got through sprucing up, it was almost six-thirty, so I left my room and rapped on the door across the hall. Jewel opened it.

"Y'all about ready for some dinner?" I asked.

"Marlene's still getting dressed. Why don't you round up the rest of the gang, and we'll meet you downstairs in a few minutes?"

I agreed and asked what room the boys were in, which turned out to be the one next door. I went and rapped on that door but got no answer. Knowing my adventurous nephews, they were probably exploring their new domain and driving Maynard Dabney's employees crazy. I went across the hall to Melissa's room and knocked. Rebecca answered the door.

"Yes?" she said, one little brown arm on her hip and a put-on snooty look on her pretty face. "May I help you?"

I bowed. "Yes, madam. Is madam ready for her din-din?"

"And what are you serving tonight, my good man?"

"Fricasseed worms with turtle gravy."

"Sounds delicious. Let me get my maid and we'll be right . . ." She burst into giggles as her "maid" came up behind her and picked her up, swinging her up in the air.

"Madam's gonna get her buns busted if she doesn't watch out!" Melissa said, tummy-gumming Rebecca's neck.

I laughed. "You two ready?" I asked.

The three of us went downstairs and towards the dining room, with me scanning the lobby for the boys. I found them by the postcard rack. "You two hungry?" I asked. Which was a dumb question. Those two boys were always hungry. Shit, they'd even eat their mama's cooking like it was good.

For some reason, coming into the Longbranch Inn's dining room from the hotel made it different from coming in the street door. The place looked different. But I still very cautiously shied away from Glenda Sue's station. We needed a big table anyway, and there wasn't one at Glenda Sue's station. Jewel and Marlene joined us after about five minutes.

I didn't order what I usually ordered at the Longbranch, which was chicken-fried steak with cream gravy, mashed potatoes, fried okra, and corn bread. To do that would have seemed like a betrayal, even though Glenda Sue never actually cooked the stuff. But who can figure guilt? So I ordered meat loaf instead. With scalloped potatoes, corn, and a roll. It was good, but not as good as my usual. The seven of us pigged out and talked, discussing the cleaning party planned for the next day. Well, the women discussed it. The boys and I just groaned with each new idea they came up with.

But then Jewel Anne said to me, "This will be a great opportunity to fix up that house."

"What's wrong with my house?" I asked, putting my fork down and looking at my sister, daring her to say what was on her mind. But she was too busy slopping food into her mouth to notice she was treading on thin ice.

"Well, Milton, you never have fixed that place up! I mean, it hasn't been painted or papered since you got there. And that kitchen!"

"What's wrong with my kitchen?" The kids all got up and left the table, but Jewel kept going.

"It's a disgrace!"

"And how do you plan on fixing *my* house up?"

Melissa's eyes darted back and forth between my sister and me, but Jewel just kept on.

"Well, for one thing I think we should paint the exterior a nice pastel...."

"Over stucco?"

"And I saw this thing in a magazine about pickled wood. It's wonderful! For a kitchen or bathroom. I was thinking a light blue for the kitchen..."

"Jesus Christ!"

"What?" Jewel said, looking up for the first time, a look of surprise on her face.

"You ain't pickling any goddamn wood in *my* house!"

Jewel frowned. "Oh, we're back onto this 'your' house business again, are we?"

So far we'd spent about twenty hours and a couple thousand dollars in Dr. Marston's office discussing what's hers and what's mine.

"You pick out the furniture, I pick out what goes permanent in the house."

"Why? I live there too, you know!"

"For the time being!"

Jewel stiffened and I knew I'd gone too far. So did Melissa. She looked from one of us to the other and said, "How about some peach cobbler for dessert?"

By eight o'clock everybody was through and ready to go upstairs. I said good night to all at the elevator and hightailed it across the street to the Katch & Scram for a six-pack of Millers Lite and a pack of Marlboros.

SEVEN

I LIT UP as I crossed the street on the way back to the hotel. I was finally getting used to smoking again and kinda missed the little buzz I'd gotten when I first started up. Now there was no buzz, just a god-awful craving, just like twenty years ago. But it was soothing too, kinda like an old friend. Someone you didn't know how much you'd missed. I figured I'd quit again, when all of this was over. But right now, I needed my old friend. Needed something to lean on, even if it was just a piece of paper wrapped around some dried leaves.

I stood on the porch of the Longbranch, sucking on my Marlboro, thinking about the terrible things my sister was going to do to my house. Pale blue pickled wood, dusty rose carpet, and fru-fras all over the goddamned place.

I finished the cigarette, ground it beneath my heel, and went into the lobby. Hearing voices coming from one of the large meeting rooms in the back of the first floor, I headed that way to investigate, not in that big an all-fired rush to go up to my empty room. And the possibility of my sister ambushing me.

There was a little marquee board by the entrance to the meeting room with letters on it saying, "Monthly Meeting—Patriots for a Free America—7 P.M.—Newcomers Welcome." I recognized that as the group I'd seen marching in the Pioneer Week parade, the guys in the white shirts, black pants, and blue gimme hats. I've never been much of a joiner, I mean I belong to the Benevolent Order of Oklahoma Peace Officers, and I pay my dues to the American Legion, but that's about my limit. But I saw no reason I couldn't sit in and see what it was all about. I stashed my six-pack in a little alcove in the hall and gingerly opened the door, finding a seat at the back.

The guys in white shirts, black slacks, and blue gimme hats were sitting in the front four rows, about twenty-five guys all told. All the rows after that were the newcomers, about ten of us, dressed like normal people.

The guy at the podium, up on the little stage, was dressed in what I supposed was the uniform, but his gimme hat was orange. I guessed he was an officer, president or something. Behind him sat four other guys in orange hats. I knew the fella behind the podium, his name was Davey Guy, and he worked as a mechanic at Ace Auto Shoppe. He worked on my '55 once. Once. He wasn't that good, and he'd never touch it again, thank you very much.

"Now if that's all the old business," he said, "I'm gonna turn the podium over to Marty Vanderhoff, who'll give you the treasurer's report. Marty?"

Marty Vanderhoff, one of the four in orange gimme hats sitting in the chairs behind the podium, stood and changed places with Davey Guy. He cleared his throat and began reading figures. Marty was produce manager at the Foodworld. I didn't know him personally, but I recognized him. "Last month's dues came to $475, giving us a total in the treasury for the year of $33,025. We had expenditures of $11.35 this month for a mailing we did and $27.32 for refreshments at the family barbecue last week. Bringing monthly expenditures to $38.67. And I'm happy to say we've received another anonymous donation of $10,000 which brings our total to date, less expenditures, to $43,461.33. That's the end of the treasurer's report."

Marty sat down and Davey came up to the podium. "Well, that's just wonderful, Marty. Thank you." He applauded and the audience joined in. "We've been blessed," Davey said, "by an anonymous donation of $10,000. There's somebody out there that knows we're doing good works. And we're thankful. Now for those of you just visiting tonight, I wanna stress that the Patriots for a Free America is just that. We're just folks who understand what our country's all about. We love our country and want to do right by it and have it do right by us. That's all we are. We're glad you could join us tonight and hope you'll take home some literature and consider becoming a part of our organization."

Davey cleared his throat and shuffled his papers. "Now tonight we got us a special treat. We're honored to have a guest speaker tonight who really needs no introduction. He's worked for this country all his life, first as a Marine in Vietnam and later as leader of many different patriotic organizations. It's with great honor that I present Mr. Chester Oliver."

Davey stepped away from the podium, and a man I hadn't noticed got up from a chair in the corner of the stage and walked forward. He was midforties, paunchy, wearing a dark suit and red tie, and his light brown hair was plastered to the crown of his head, obviously covering a bald spot. I applauded with the rest of the audience.

"Hi, fellas," he started. "It's great to be in the great state of Oklahoma."

The members in the front rows burst into applause and stood up, shouting and stomping. After a minute, being smiled upon by Mr. Oliver, they sat and began quieting down.

"And Oklahoma *is* a great state! Though it's been hurt lately, God knows. And hurt by what? Lazy Okies who don't know how to earn a dollar? Who'd rather live off welfare than put food on their families' tables like men?"

The members grumbled.

"No. I don't think so. I *know* that's not so!"

There were responses in the audience of "That's right!" and "Yeah, you got it!"

Oliver was quiet for a moment, his gaze seeking out people in the audience individually. Finally, he said, "What's hurting Oklahoma has nothing to do with the people of this fair state. It's got nothing to do with how hard they work and how much they want to provide for their families. What's hurting the great state of Oklahoma is a bunch of camel jockeys halfway around the world telling *us* what price we gotta sell *our* oil!"

The members stood up at that, clapping and shouting "Yeah!" "Ain't that the truth!" and hooting and hollering.

When the members had sat back down and quieted some, Oliver let his gaze roam around the room again. Finally, in a real quiet voice, he said, "It's getting to be in this country that a white man has no rights."

"Yeah," somebody shouted.

"The luckiest person in the world for getting a job these days is a *black woman*," he said, "because that fills *two* government requirements!"

Grumble, grumble.

"I don't begrudge the employer! He's just some guy trying to put food on *his* family's table. But he's got to abide by what the *government* tells him to do! And the *government* is telling him he's gotta have so many blacks and so many Mexicans and so many women.... But the government doesn't *never* tell him how many *white men* to hire!"

Somebody in the front row jumped up and shouted, "Ain't that the goddamn truth!" Then they all commenced to hooting and hollering.

"I'm tired," Oliver said. "Tired of apologizing for being a man. Tired of apologizing for being white! Tired of seeing them *Negroes* driving around in better cars than I can afford just to pick up their food stamps!"

Everybody was standing now, including me (so I could see over everybody's heads), and most were shouting amens and hallelujahs.

"I'm tired of *my* government giving wetbacks a free ride. I'm tired of *my* government putting food on the tables of the niggers and spics and taking farms away from my brothers!"

The whole place exploded in applause and shouts and whistles, and I moved out to the aisle, heading to the door. On the way there, I passed a table covered with handouts. I grabbed one and headed out the door and over to my six-pack, 'cause the one thing Mr. Oliver's speech inspired in me was the need for a beer.

I went on up to my quiet, empty room and laid down on the bed, lighting up a cigarette and popping the top on a cold one. The handout I'd grabbed was a newspaper of sorts, something called the White Gazette, for God's sake. And perusing it, I couldn't believe my eyes. I hadn't seen shit like this since I was a little kid, back after WWII when people were resenting blacks coming home from the war and wanting jobs like real people.

The front page article wasn't on race, though. It was all about how all this glasnost stuff was a Communist plot to take over America. How they had proof (proof, mind you) that the Soviets had hundreds of miles of underground bunkers filled with atom bombs, and the stuff they were declaring to get rid of in the arms talks was all just junk left over from WWII. This was front page stuff.

Now on page two, there was a very interesting article. All about how their ''scientists'' had proved that the sexual contact of a white woman with a black man can result in the woman having black babies, even if she later has sex with a white man and the white man is the father. The article said that it "has long been a known fact" that if a white woman had a baby by a black man, that her next baby, fathered by a white man, would be black. Something semitechnical about black chromosomes sticking to the sides of the womb, or some such shit.

But now they've discovered, these scientists of theirs, that the woman didn't even have to have a black man's baby first. All she had to do was have sex with one. All that black stuff'll just stay up there and come out all over the baby.

Not only that, but once a white woman engages in sex with a black man, she should no longer be considered part of the white race. It was interesting all through there how white was spelled with a capital W and Negro was spelled with a small n. Anyway, according to their scientists, just having sex with a black man caused a mental change in a white woman, and she would tend to become "pronegro" and "prorace mixing" because she now has "Negro" chemicals racing through her body. The article ended with the warning that "The difference between the races is so great that any large-scale interbreeding between the races would bring about the actual downfall of civilization it-self.''

I decided I'd had enough reading for my evening. I snuffed out my cigarette, got up with the paper and my lighter, and went to the bathroom, burning the White Gazette in the sink and washing the ashes down the drain.

And then I went back to my bed and laid down and drank my beer and thought. And I thought. I thought about what I'd just read and what Oliver had said and about my new grandbaby in the room next door.

I never had thought much about how I felt about what you might call the race situation. We don't have many blacks in Prophesy County, and I guess them we got is what you might call the Uncle Tom kind. Menial laborers who say ''yes, sir'' a lot. Of course, I didn't know what they said when they got home and Whitey wasn't around. Being in the Air Force, I was around blacks some then, but never thought about it much. They stuck to themselves. I stuck with the white guys from the South 'cause they were easier to talk to than the white yankees. I never considered myself a bigot. And I'm able to spot one a mile off. I've always kinda looked down on bigots, knowing they're mostly just ignorant people who don't know much better.

But now I had a reason to really look into my heart. Into how I felt. I guess all of us, underneath, are prejudiced to some extent. But I'd never really had to look at it before. I'd never had an adopted grandbaby whose daddy was black before, either. And how did I feel about that? How did I feel about the fact that if her own blood-grandpa had called her a little nigger, how many others were going to?

All of a sudden, I realized that little Rebecca was more important to me than anybody who'd ever been in my life before. I wanted more than anything to watch her grow up healthy and strong and unhurt. But I also knew that could never happen. In a perfect world it could, but this was anything but a perfect world. There were a hell of a lot of Olivers out there, spewing their venom, and for every one of them, there were another fifty who'd listen and take it to heart. Right here in the same hotel where my little Rebecca slept were a score of men who'd do her harm because of the color of her skin. I got to thinking maybe Melissa should leave Oklahoma, go back to California, raise Rebecca there. Maybe for all its craziness and faddishness and weird religions and all the other, maybe there was room in California for a little half-black half-white girl to grow up okay.

Somehow, with all that on my mind, I managed to fall asleep with a cigarette in my hand and burn a hole in my only shirt.

"He knocked me up."

I sit on the bleachers with Glenda Sue, watching the team work out. I'm not playing this week since my foot's still in a cast. We sit there side by side, watching the best quarterback the Longbranch Cougars ever had run his plays.

"Shit," I say in response.

"Shit is right. Now what do I do?"

"You tell him?"

She shakes her head.

"You want me to marry you?"

Glenda Sue laughs. "Miss LaDonna'd get pretty pissed off about that, don't you think?"

I shrug. "Whatju gonna do?"

She looks at me, shielding her eyes against the sun, then looks away. "I heard about a guy over in Ardmore. Mary Anne's cousin went to him. Cost two hundred dollars."

"Where you gonna get two hundred dollars?"

She shrugged. "I dunno. Sell my body?"

"Well, you sure as hell couldn't get in any more trouble doing that."

She hits me on the arm. "Funny as a dead dog, Milt."

"You gotta tell Linn."

We both look to the field, watching him strut his stuff.

"You think he's gonna give up that OU scholarship to make an honest woman of me?"

I shrug. "You never can tell."

The phone rang, just as I was stepping on the escalator. I woke up with a start, wondering what this new wrinkle was in the dream. When I realized it was the phone and that I was actually awake, I sighed with relief and fumbled the phone to my ear. "What?" I said.

"We picked up Kretcher and Bass," Emmett's voice said.

"Where are they?"

"Lockup."

"I'm on my way."

Emmett must have left his house in a hurry, I noticed when I walked down the steps to the basement holding cells, 'cause he still had on the tops to his pajamas. Had a cute little pattern of clocks, all of 'em reading midnight. I myself sleep in my underwear and have never owned a pair of pajamas in my adult life. I wondered about the powers in law enforcement in this town that they ran to cute pj's.

"Emmett," I called, and he turned around.

"Well, looky what we got us here, Milt."

I stood next to Emmett and looked in the cell, and sure enough, there they lay, Doyle Kretcher and Lamar Bass.

"Where'd you find 'em?" I asked.

"Paul Riverwater caught 'em running the light on College."

"One light in this goddamn town, and you run it, huh?" I said to the cell. It didn't answer me. But then again, I never really expected it to. "So, they were right here in Longbranch."

"Looks like it," Emmett answered.

"You think they was here when my house got broken into?" I asked.

"Coulda been."

"You think they were here when Glenda Sue's trailer got broken into?" I asked.

Emmett nodded. "Seems likely."

"You think they was here when Glenda Sue Robinson's throat got slashed?"

Emmett shrugged. "Could be..."

Two bodies popped outta the bunks and hit cell bars. "Now wait just a goddamn minute..." Lamar Bass started.

"We don't know nothing about no murder!" Doyle piped in.

"How'd you know it was murder?" Emmett asked.

Bass snorted. "Like somebody slashed their own throat on accident?"

Bass had a point and Emmett knew it, so he let it go. Instead, he gave them the date of Glenda Sue's murder. "Where were you two that night and the next day? That was the day you jumped bail if you need some point of reference."

"We were down to Sherman," Bass said. "My old lady lives in Sherman."

"Your wife?" Emmett asked.

"No, man, we ain't married. We got a kid, but she's just my old lady."

"Well, I got me an ugly habit of not believing the wives and girlfriends and 'old ladies' of scumbags like you. I figure they stupid enough to hook up with you, they stupid enough not to know the day of the week. Anybody else seen you in Sherman?"

They looked at each other, then Doyle grinned. "Yeah, the Sherman police. I got stopped about two o'clock Saturday morning 'cause them Texas police don't like looking at Oklahoma tags."

I turned around and walked out. I knew Emmett would check it out, and somehow I knew it would check out true. Which left me with exactly nothing to go on, 'cause as far as Dr. Jim had been able to figure out, Glenda Sue had died somewhere between midnight and 3:00 A.M. And since it's a three-hour drive to Sherman from here, even if you break a few speed laws, I figured that put the scumbags in the clear. I went back to the hotel and tried to go back to sleep.

The next morning I called the sheriff and begged a sick day. I told the gang I'd meet 'em at the house, then hightailed it over to Kanter's Department Store to the men's department. I bought their entire stock of white oxford cloth shirts in my size, which came to three, bought two pairs of jeans, a sweatshirt with OU emblazoned on the chest, and my first pair of running pants. I didn't plan on running in 'em, but they sure were comfortable.

Back at the hotel, I dressed in the running pants and sweatshirt and made my way as slowly as my conscience would allow to the house on Mountain Falls Road.

Nowadays, my house is the only one being lived in on Mountain Falls Road. After the tornado and a run-in with a developer who was trying to buy up the mountain for time-share condos, my part-time neighbor, Billie Moulini, bought up everybody who wanted to sell. Which was everybody but me. After the tornado one house had been ruined and then torn down, and the campground/trailer court at the bottom of the falls had also been demolished. So now the only houses were mine, Billie's mountain cabin château that he hardly ever used, and old Mrs. Munsky's farmhouse that had been sitting empty since her body was hauled off after her murder a while back.

There was a "for rent" sign on the Munsky farmhouse, but so far I was still all alone with my family on my mountain. And most of the time, I kinda liked it that way. Felt sorta like a feudal lord, looking out my windows and pretending I owned everything I saw. High up on my mountain looking down on the little people. But I didn't have regiments of serfs and serfettes to protect my loved ones. Didn't have a moat and a drawbridge to keep my people safe while I was away fighting my wars.

If we lived in town, on a little street with old-lady neighbors, what had happened to Jewel and Rebecca would have been seen and reported immediately, and Rebecca wouldn't have had to spend more than a minute in that cold, damp cellar. Hell, we might have caught the vandals in the act, if we'd had old-lady neighbors staring out their window shades. Instead, we were isolated up here on my mountain, isolated and alone. For the first time ever, my mountain wasn't the haven I'd always thought it to be.

"I said let me out of the goddamn car!" Glenda Sue grabs the door handle and tries to push the door open. Linn hits the accelerator, pushing the old Ford to 90 mph. From the backseat I grab

Glenda Sue by the shoulders, trying to keep her in the car.

LaDonna punches me on the leg. "Just stay out of it!" she hisses.

I look at LaDonna, while still holding onto Glenda Sue, wanting to save my friend's life and pacify my woman at the same time. Finally, Glenda Sue lets the pressure of the wind close the door, and I let go of her shoulders. Two seconds later, Linn slams on the brakes and pulls the car to the side of the road.

"You want out, get the fuck out!"

"Oh, I'll get the fuck out! Don't worry about that!" Glenda Sue screams, opening the door and jumping out.

"Glen!" I yell. "Linn, man . . . y'all cool it."

Linn punches the accelerator, and we spew gravel getting back on the blacktop. Looking out the back window, I see that it hits Glenda Sue, pelting her like buckshot.

"Man, you're gonna put her eye out!"

"Fuck off, Kovak!"

He's hitting the accelerator hard, the speedometer closing in on 80 mph, 90, 100, 120. . . .

I look at LaDonna, who's crying silently against my shoulder. "Jesus," I think. "It all used to be so easy."

I pulled up in the driveway, parking behind Jewel's station wagon, and got out of the '55. Inside I could hear the industry going on, the sounds of the kids arguing with Jewel, the sounds of trash being hauled and carpets being vacuumed. I walked in and saw them all in the living room, everybody doing a job, even little Rebecca.

"Hey, y'all," I greeted.

"Grab the broom," Jewel ordered, "and get started in the entry hall. If you see anything that's whole, put it on the back porch."

So I set about doing as I was told. All alone, just me and my thoughts.

"She's preggers."

"That's what I hear," I say.

Linn gives me one of those looks. The kind he gives to an end who drops an easy pass. *"She tell you?"*

"Yeah, she did. Why?"

I shrug.

"Maybe 'cause it might be yours?"

"Shit," I say.

"Well?"

"No way, man."

He shrugs. *"Could be anybody's,"* he says.

"Linn . . ."

"Who knows who the bitch's been fuckin'?"

"Linn...man, you're it and you know it. Glenny ain't that way."

Again he shrugs. "She's gonna have a hell of time proving it."

Half an hour later, Jewel and I ended up in the dining room, staring at the china cabinet that had housed our mama's china and crystal, now laying broken and shattered on the floor.

"I can't stand this," Jewel said, a sob caught in her throat.

I put my arm around my little sister's shoulders. "I know, honey," I said. "I know."

Jewel finagled her way down to the floor and began sorting through the mess. After a minute I joined her. Her tears were flowing freely, and I wished for a minute I was a liberated kinda fella myself so I could join her. Here we were, on the floor, sorting through the shards of my mama's Thanksgivings and Christmases. My mama's special anniversary dinners and birthday treats. My mama's Sunday dinners with the preacher. Every special day and special meal of my childhood was broken on the floor of the dining room. And if that's not enough to make a grown man cry, then I don't rightly know what is.

Melissa and the kids were upstairs, working in the bedrooms, letting Jewel and I handle the dining room and the memories. After about twenty minutes, Jewel said, "Look!" Triumphantly, she held up the sugar bowl to Mama's china set. The bowl and the little lid were intact.

"Well, I'll be goddamn!" I said, grinning.

"Maybe there's more," Jewel cried.

Feverishly, the two of us crawled around the floor. After it was all over, we found the sugar bowl, two saucers, and one cup from the china, and one crystal dessert plate intact. To us it was a king's ransom. A pirate's treasure hoard. *Something* of Mama's whole. *Something* of Mama's to pass on down the line, from Jewel to Marlene to Marlene's children and on. *Something*.

By the end of the day, the back porch was filled to overflowing with the things we'd salvaged. Clothes that could be saved with a washing, books that had escaped slashing, five record albums that had been stuffed under Leonard's bed and had escaped the terror and destruction, pots and pans and silverware, Tupperware that even vandals couldn't destroy (I mean, that's hardy stuff!), a couple of chairs, an ottoman, some linens, the Water Pik (hallelujah!), and a half a ton of other assorted crap.

But not enough for a family of seven, which is what we were now. Not enough crap to make life worth living for a modern family of seven.

Jewel used the only phone still in working order and called Chuck Lancaster in Houston and told him he could have his claims adjuster come on out and have a look. Then I called Lucille Bright and told her the same thing. She didn't seem as interested as Chuck, and I thought about maybe changing my insurance agent. I mean after all, I was pretty damned sure I was gonna get canceled anyway.

Chuck called back after half an hour and said the claims adjuster would be out in a couple of days, that he'd call Jewel at the Longbranch and make an appointment. After that we left, heading back to town and dinner at the Longbranch.

EIGHT

I SAT UP with a start, gasping for breath. God-damn dream. It didn't seem to want to go away. Every night now I woke up from the same damned dream. The cobblestone floor, the escalator, Rebecca standing at the top, and those god-awful woman legs with the braces and the sensible shoes. If I could just go beyond that, past the woman's hand reaching for Rebecca and Rebecca walking away with her. If I could just get to the top and follow them. Find out what was going on. Find out why I was so goddamned scared.

I reached for a cigarette and lit up. Then I popped the top on a lukewarm Lite and guzzled half of it in a swallow. My T-shirt was soaked through with sweat. I got up and changed, going to the bathroom and splashing some cold water on my face. Every night now. Every night since the night Glenda Sue died, I'd had the dream. I was getting maybe four or five hours of sleep a night. And this for a guy who could do ten without a piss break. I was running on half-empty and I knew it.

I crawled back into bed, turned off the light, and lay there, staring at the ceiling and listening to the hum of the Longbranch Inn's central heating system. It was old and crotchety and made noises in the night. Just like me.

I woke up at seven to the sound of my alarm, rolled over, threw the thing across the room, and went back to sleep. At seven-thirty, Melissa woke me up banging on the door.

"Milt, we gotta go! You up?"

"Um . . ."

"Come on, old man! Get the lead out! Rise and shine! Get a move on!"

"Drop dead."

The door knob rattled. "Milton!" she called in a singsong voice. "Get up now before I wake up the entire hotel!"

I pulled myself out of bed and went to the door in my shorts, opening it and falling back into bed. Melissa came in. I could see her out of the corner of my eye. She was standing there sorta sideways, her hands on her hips, dressed and ready for work.

"This is my first day on the job, Milt. I don't want to be late. I don't want to get fired on my first day. I like to reserve that distinction for my second day. Okay? You said you'd drive me. Now are you going to get up, or am I going to have to get a bucket of water and pour it in your ear?"

"Go away."

"You've got nice legs," she said, moving towards the bed and pulling one of my nice legs onto the floor. "I'd hate to have to break one."

I sat up and held my head in my hands. "Go downstairs and have breakfast. Order me an English muffin to go. I'll be down in a minute."

"Can I trust you?" she asked.

"No," I answered.

She sighed. "If you're not going to drive me, tell me now so I can go wake up Jewel and have her drive me."

"All right, all right." I got up and moved towards the bathroom. "I'm moving."

"Okay. I'll go downstairs."

"Yeah. English muffin. To go. And black coffee."

"Okay." I heard the door shut on her tentative farewell. The girl didn't trust me. But who could blame her?

Twenty minutes later I was pulling my '55 into the parking lot of the Longbranch Memorial Hospital. "Why don't you park and come up?" Melissa suggested. "I'd love for you to meet Dr. McDonnell."

"Sure," I said, not really wanting to but always one to do what's requested of me by the females in my life, rather than have to live with the consequences.

"Psst . . . Milt!"

I turn from my nervous stance at the entrance to the sanctuary and see Glenda Sue's head sticking out the door to the choir room, her blonde hair done up in a modified beehive, a rhinestone tiara and veil perched on top. I move quickly to the door to the choir room. Glenda Sue grabs my arm and pulls me inside. Her mother and her cousin Ruth are in the room with her. She's wearing only her bra and a set of full petticoats.

"Mama, you and Ruth go on out now."

"Glenda Sue! You don't bring this boy in here dressed like that!"

"Mama, it's okay! It's just Milt!"

I don't know whether to laugh or cry. "Hey, Miz Rainey," I say.

Mrs. Rainey's mouth goes all pruney as she looks at me. "Milton," she says, then storms out of the room, cousin Ruth on her heels.

"What?" I ask Glenda Sue, trying not to look at her breasts poking out of her bra.

"You really think I should do this?" she says, lifting herself up to sit atop the choir director's desk. Her petticoats fly upward, covering her almost to her chin.

"Do what?"

"Get married, asshole!"

I snort. "Don't you think it's a little late to back out now?"

Glenda Sue sticks three rolled up pieces of Juicy Fruit in her mouth and begins chewing. Around the gum, she says, "Ain't never too late for nothin'."

I shrug. "Well, you're the one's gotta make that decision."

"Linn show up?"

"Yeah, he's in the bathroom."

"Doin' what?"

I laugh. "Puking his guts up."

Glenda Sue smiled. "Goddamn," she says. "That's sweet."

I parked and followed Melissa into the hospital and into the elevator. On the third floor, we got off and headed down the hall, past the nurse's station and up to a locked door with a guard. The new psychiatric wing of the hospital. Makes you feel real secure knowing Longbranch now has a wing of the hospital that has to be locked and guarded.

"That's there mainly for the detox cases," Melissa explained as the guard checked her ID and unlocked the door. "I mean," she said, "it's not like we've got raving lunatics in here. Just some depression cases, an attempted suicide or two, and the drug and alcohol patients."

"Um . . ." I said.

"You're not getting all judgmental, are you?"

"Who me?" I was offended. "Judgmental? I haven't got a judgmental bone in my body!"

"Um . . ." she said, as she stopped in front of a desk with a lady sitting at it. "Hi," Melissa said, "I'm Melissa Robinson. I'm supposed to start today."

The woman smiled and extended her hand. "Bette Raintree. I must have been at lunch when you interviewed with Dr. McDonnell. I'm her secretary."

"It's nice to meet you. Is she in? Dr. McDonnell?"

"Yes, and she wanted to see you as soon as you got here." Bette Raintree looked at me.

"Oh," Melissa said, "this is my . . . stepfather. I wanted him to meet Dr. McDonnell."

Ms. Raintree smiled at both of us. A pretty smile on a pretty, round, Indian face. She stood up and walked us to a door behind her desk, knocked, opened it, and announced us, ushering us inside and closing the door behind us.

Dr. McDonnell was sitting at a desk by the window. She was an attractive woman in her midforties, with reddish-brown hair with a few strands of gray, cut simply. Her smile when she greeted Melissa showed a mouthful of straight teeth and dimples in rosy cheeks. Her eyes were green-blue and sparkled. A very attractive woman.

"It's great to have you with us, Melissa," she said. Then seeing me, she raised an eyebrow. One eyebrow. I always wished I could do that. My mama could. Raise one eyebrow, I mean. Whenever I said something she found particularly stupid.

"This is my stepfather, Milton Kovak. I wanted him to meet you. I hope it's okay?"

Dr. McDonnell smiled and stood up, walking around the desk. "Certainly. It's a pleasure, Mr. Kovak..."

She stopped talking because I had fallen back onto the sofa in her office and was staring at her. Staring at her legs. Her feet in their sensible shoes and the braces that went from there up under the hem of her skirt.

"Milt!" Melissa said, her voice sharp.

"Mr. Kovak? Are you all right?" Dr. McDonnell asked.

"Excuse me, I'm not feeling too well," I said, getting shakily to my feet. "I'd better go...."

I turned and walked out as quickly as my shaking legs could carry me, oblivious to what had to be some strange looks coming my way.

Once back in my car, I sat there for a long time, trying to figure out what had just happened. Dr. McDonnell was a dream come true, all right, but not the right kind. Was this just a coincidence? Of

course it was, how could it be otherwise? Melissa
working for a lady with braces on her legs had
nothing to do with me dreaming about Rebecca
being in trouble with a lady with braces on her legs.
It was stupid. I've never been one to take much
stock in second sight, or ESP, or any of that horse
hockey. So how could I take seriously a recurring
dream? That's all it was. Just a stupid recurring
dream, and it was just a coincidence that Dr.
McDonnell had a resemblance to someone in that
dream.

"Ouija, am I going to be a famous actress?"

"This is stupid," I say, holding on to my end of
the platen.

"Shut up, Milt!" Glenda Sue hisses. *"Oh, ouija,
answer please!"*

"This is the dumbest thing..."

*All of a sudden we hear a strange sound. A voice
coming out of nowhere. "No, you will not be a famous actress. You will marry a garage mechanic
and have seven children."*

*Then Linn falls out from behind the sofa where
he's been hiding, laughing so hard he has to hold
his sides. Glenda Sue is not amused.*

I felt like an idiot for the way I'd acted and
hoped I hadn't ruined Melissa's job opportunity. I
started the car and drove to the station, embarrassed, chagrined, and all that other stuff.

When I got there, to the station, Gladys greeted me with a "while you were out" slip. "Call Melissa" it said and gave a number. Wonderful. I went into my office, shut the door, and dialed.

"What in the hell was that all about?" Melissa asked as soon as I had her on the line.

"Sorry. I wasn't feeling too good."

"Bullshit." There was a silence. Then she said, "Are you going to tell me?"

I'm having this recurring dream where your daughter's in danger and your boss is the one who's doing it. Yeah, right, I was really gonna tell her that. "Nothing to tell, honey. I apologize. I just wasn't feeling well."

"Are you always this weird, Milt, or is this something new?"

"No, honey, I'm always this weird."

"Well, at least you're consistent. See you at dinner."

"Okay. Bye."

I sat back in my chair and stared at the ceiling, wondering when life was gonna get okay again.

"When did it all go so bad?" Glenda Sue asks me.

I sit with her in the emergency room, waiting for the young intern neither of us know to show up and do something. Mend the broken lip, kiss the bruised eye.

I pat her shoulder, knowing it's a futile gesture. "I don't know, Glenny. Why don't you tell me?"

"Don't call me Glenny."

"Sorry."

We sit for a moment, not knowing or not wanting to say, I'm not sure which.

Finally, I ask, "When did he start this shit?"

Glenda Sue laughs, "On our wedding night."

I look at her strangely. She shrugs. "Well, we'd done everything else. I guess he needed something to make our wedding night special."

As soon as my door opened, I knew the answer to my question. Not in any goddamned hurry. Because standing in my doorway, a grim look on his face, was Kenneth Marshallton, the assistant county attorney, the last person in the world I wanted to see. Ever.

"Kovak," he said, sliding in and setting his rump down on my desk.

"Kenny," I said, imitating the sheriff in a way I knew would piss him off.

"Got any leads on your girlfriend?" he asked with a smirk. Smarmy little bastard.

"We're working on it."

"Yeah. I bet."

"What can I do for you, Kenny?"

"Well, you can start by telling me why you look better for this thing than anybody else we got, Kovak."

"Maybe 'cause you ain't looking too hard, Kenny."

Again he smirked. "Show me somebody else to look at, I'll look."

I was beginning to fight a rage building up inside me. I didn't need this. I didn't need this asshole coming in and accusing me of the horrible things that had happened to Glenda Sue.

I stood up, leaning my weight on my arms on the desk. "Look, you little assho..."

"Kenny, how you doing?" the sheriff said from the doorway.

Marshallton and I both looked his direction. Marshallton stood up, relieving my desk of his shiny red ass.

"Elberry."

"What can we do for you?"

"Just checking on what you have on the Robinson killing."

"Milt tell you we got us some leads we're following up?"

"No."

Turning to me, the sheriff said, "Now, Milt, we gotta be open with the county attorney's office, you know that." Slipping an arm around Kenny's shoulders, the sheriff led him gently to the door. "Well, Kenny, the thing is . . ."

The door closed behind the two, and I sat down, counted to ten, and did a little deep breathing. And was still pissed as hell when I was through.

But my morning wasn't over yet. All my problems and dilemmas were just beginning. I knew that the minute the door opened again, and I saw Dr. McDonnell walk in, arms hooked in the rings of shiny aluminum crutches.

"May I come in, Mr. Kovak?" she asked.

I stood up. "Yes, ma'am. Please do."

I indicated a chair, and she sat down, resting the crutches next to the chair. "There was no one at the front desk, so I just followed the signs. I hope I didn't break any laws."

"No, ma'am." I sat down. Cleared my throat. Looked at the wall behind her.

"I'm sorry if I made you uncomfortable this morning. Most people don't have quite that violent a reaction to my handicap. Repulsion, pity, ambivalence, but rarely fear, Mr. Kovak."

"It's not . . ." I cleared my throat again. "It's not . . ." I stared at the wall again. "I apologize, Dr. McDonnell. I don't want you to think . . ."

"What, Mr. Kovak?"

So what could I do? I told her. All of it. The first dream. Glenda Sue's murder. The recurrence of the dream. The change in the dream from some anonymous little boy to Rebecca.

When I'd finished, she smiled. "I must have scared the shit out of you."

I smiled back. "Yes, ma'am, you did."

"Do you have any idea what these dreams are signifying?"

I shook my head. "All I know is something is wrong.... I don't know...."

"Children or babies in dreams often mean creation. New beginnings. You say you asked Glenda Sue to marry you that night, is that right?"

"Yes."

"And she declined. So your new beginning with her was in jeopardy. The next day you find out she's been brutally murdered. Your new beginning with her has been crushed. Hence the fear. When the anonymous little boy changes to Melissa's daughter, it may be because you now have a child's face to place in your dream. Your fears are still there, maybe because you haven't resolved yourself to Glenda Sue's death as yet. That takes time. Healing time. I will suggest to you that as your wounds heal, as you go through the grieving process, these dreams will lessen."

"You think so?"

"I'm certain." She smiled at me, and I smiled back. "We sometimes use medications to block

REM sleep, which is when you dream. We don't want to do this for any length of time because you need REM sleep to be fully rested. But if you want, I'll give you a small prescription for some potent sleeping pills.''

I shook my head. ''Thanks, but I feel better just talking about it. I have a feeling I'll sleep soundly tonight.''

Dr. McDonnell stood up, and I joined her, noticing as I did so that she was at least two inches taller than me. Making her well over six foot. Big woman. Big, good-looking woman. I held out my hand, and she shook it. She had a cool, tight grasp. Then she let go and fitted the crutches on her arms.

''Thanks . . .'' I said.

She turned at the door. ''You're welcome. We can't have the keepers of peace in our community suffering from lack of sleep. I consider this a public service.'' She laughed, a light, tinkling sound, and left.

Of course, she never did mention the ''coincidence'' of the woman legs. Never mentioned it at all.

NINE

ME AND Linn stand with our hands on our hips, staring down at the girl sitting on the step.

"I want my marbles back," Linn says.

She looks up, squinting at the sun behind our backs. "What marbles?" she says.

"The ones you took yesterday."

"I didn't take nothin'," she says. "I won them marbles fair and square."

"Give me my marbles," Linn says, gritting his teeth. "Or I'll hit you!"

I put my hand on Linn's shoulder. "You can't hit her," I whisper. "She's a girl."

The girl stands up. "You try it, pus brain! I'll knock your rotten teeth out!"

"She sure don't act like a girl!" Linn says, moving toward her with his fist raised.

I move between the two of them. "Let's play her again," I say. "Win those marbles back. We weren't playing our best yesterday 'cause she's a girl."

Glenda Sue Rainey smiles. "You got some more marbles?" she asks.

Around four-thirty I got a call from Gladys at the front desk saying Kenneth Marshallton was back to see me.

"I left by the back door five minutes ago, Gladys, sorry," I said.

"Milton, he hears me here talking to you."

"Gladys, you gotta stop this habit you got of talking to empty phone lines." I hung up and skedaddled out the back entrance and headed for the Longbranch. If there was anything I didn't need at the moment, it was the county attorney telling me again how good I looked as a suspect. I didn't need that at all. Not on the amount of sleep I'd been getting. I might take a swing at him this time. And miss.

My baby sister, Jewel, was in the lobby when I walked in, in animated, arm-waving conversation with Harmon Monk. I tried tiptoeing through so as not to be noticed, but Jewel Anne's never been one to miss a trick.

"Milton!" she said, jumping up and coming over to me. Harmon sat where he was, his face clouded over, his hands making fists on the arm-rests of his chair.

"Hey, Jewel," I said, then waving slightly at Harmon, I said, "Hey, Harmon." He nodded.

Harmon Monk was in love with my sister. Not an easy thing to be. And he had been since he was nineteen and she was sixteen. Between then and now, my daddy had grounded Jewel from seeing Harmon, he'd sent me over to Harmon's daddy's half-assed pig farm to warn him off, Harmon had joined the Army and gone to Vietnam, and both he and Jewel had married, to other people. Jewel went off to Houston with her husband Henry, and Harmon came back to Prophesy County where he managed to turn his daddy's half-assed pig farm into a car graveyard. And at some point, he married Leona Pritchett, the Oklahoma City socialite daughter of a man who earned his millions making coffin linings. At the moment, Harmon had eleven used auto parts yards all over this end of the state. And he was a rich man.

When Jewel's husband was killed in Houston and I brought her and the kids back to Prophesy County to live, Harmon had shown up, said "hidy," and went home and divorced his wife. Now here they were, sitting in the lobby of the Longbranch Inn, him pissed and her worried. Ain't love grand?

"What's going on, Jewel?"

"Harmon."

"I can see Harmon. What's the problem?"

"He wants the kids and me to move in with him."

"He wants what?"

"You heard me!"

"That's not what I meant, and you damn well know it, Jewel Anne!" Harmon spoke up, close to my elbow.

I turned to him. "Evening, Harmon."

"All I said was this hotel isn't a fittin' place for her and the kids to be, and that I got all that room over in Bishop. I was not implying anything... compromising."

I turned to Jewel. "Well?"

"This whole town would come unglued, and you both know it!"

"I don't give a rat's ass what this town has to say!" Harmon said. "I never have, and I never will!"

Harmon turned to me. "Milton, I wasn't proposing anything improper."

"I understand that, Harmon," I said, playing mediator.

"But you just can't tell what kind of riffraff's around a place like this. I don't like it."

"I'm right across the hall from her room, Harmon. Nothing's gonna happen to Jewel."

"That's right," Jewel piped up. "My brother, the sheriff's deputy, and his gun are right across the hall in case some lust-crazed horde decides to come breaking down my door!"

"You're making light of this, Jewel Anne," Harmon said, a long-suffering look on his face. He didn't know how long-suffering. This was just the beginning.

Seemed like I was always butting into my sister's business, but seemed like she was always asking. "Harmon," I said, "I think maybe it might be best if Jewel and the kids stayed here. Less talk, like she said, and besides, I'm right here."

Harmon's body stiffened and he gained about a half inch in height, which made him about a quarter inch taller than me for a minute or two. "Okay, then I'm getting a room here too," he said.

Jewel Anne threw up her hands and stormed towards the elevators with me and Harmon looking after her. I noticed Marigold Nail stop her and hand her the desk phone.

"What am I supposed to do with that woman?" Harmon asked me.

I shook my head. I was the wrong person to ask about any woman, let alone my baby sister. After a minute Jewel Anne joined us. "That was the claims adjuster on the phone. We're supposed to meet him tomorrow."

"You don't need me, do you?" I asked. "It's the insurance for your stuff, right?"

"This guy's working for both yours and mine. He'll do the whole house, fixtures, and furniture."

"What time?"

"Nine."

"Okay," I said.

"Do you need me to go too?" Harmon asked.

"What for?" Jewel shot back, then headed once again for the elevator.

I patted Harmon on the shoulder in sympathy and followed Jewel.

"I didn't say that," I say and sigh.

"I get sick of you always saying you didn't say what you said! And I'm sick to death of your goddamn sighs!" Glenda Sue says.

"Well, sounds to me like you're just sick to death of me!" I say.

"You said it, I didn't."

We stare at each other. Her in her half-slip and bra, one sneaker still on from work, me with my shirt unbuttoned.

"Maybe I should just go home," I say.

Glenda Sue takes off the other sneaker and throws it across the trailer. "Maybe you should."

"It's your choice," I say.

"Why do I have to make every decision around here?" she screams.

I think, "Because if I did, you'd get mad," but I don't say it. I never say it.

The next morning I woke up realizing I'd slept the whole night through. Either I hadn't had the dream, or I was too damned tired for it to wake me up. I called the office and told them I'd be in late, due to having to go meet with the claims adjuster, then went down to the restaurant and had a big, leisurely breakfast. At eight-thirty, Jewel, Rebecca, and I headed for Mountain Falls Road.

The man was waiting for us when we got there. His name was Earle Masters and he lived in Tejas County and was an independent adjuster, working for several different agencies.

He shook my hand, then Jewel's. "It's nice to meet you, Mrs. Kovak."

"Mrs. Hotchkiss," Jewel corrected.

"She's my sister," I explained, which maybe I shouldn't have.

Earle Masters's grasp of the situation was quick, and he sized my sister up as a single woman immediately. Taking her by the arm, he walked her towards the house, with Rebecca and me following.

He was well over six feet, good-looking in a smarmy kind of way. Black hair slicked back, a fashionable two-day growth of beard on his manly chin, baggy pants, and a baggy suit jacket with a

T-shirt underneath, all very Miami Vice. I didn't have the heart to tell him the show'd been canceled.

Once in the living room, surveying the damage, he said, "Jewel, can I call you Jewel?"

My sister smiled, the traitor, and said, "Certainly, Earle."

I felt like sticking my finger down my throat but resisted the urge to regurge.

"I'm so sorry this happened to you," Earle said, rubbing my sister's arm. I remembered one phone still worked and thought about calling Harmon. Have him get his shiny red ass over here.

"Well, I just hope we'll get enough to replace everything," Jewel said, smiling sweetly. I wondered how far she'd go to get her couch replaced.

Finally, we got down to business and took Earle through the house, he and my sister talking and giggling together, touching every so often. Rebecca skipped around, unmindful of the fool her Auntie Jewel was making of herself, while I followed and fumed.

When it was over, he didn't even offer us cigarettes, just shook my hand and had Jewel walk to the car with him. As he drove out of sight, I walked up to Jewel and asked, "You think Harmon might mind you bedding this guy down for furniture?"

She whirled. "What are you talking about?"

"You two make a date?"

"What business is that of yours?"

"None of mine, but Harmon . . . now that's another matter."

"I owe Harmon Monk nothing."

"Oh, really?"

"Besides, I was just being nice to that guy so he'd give us a good estimate."

"Um huh," I said, walking to my '55. I drove Jewel and Rebecca back to the hotel, my sister and I saying nothing to each other, just playing with Rebecca on the way back.

"I wasn't flirting with him," Glenda Sue says.

"I never said you were," I say.

"You implied it!" she says, her voice rising.

"If you'd rather be with a half-drunk, very married trucker than me, Glenda Sue, I ain't about to stop you!"

"I knew it! You're jealous!"

"Ha! I haven't got a jealous bone in my body! I just can't abide seeing you make an ass of yourself," I say, instantly knowing I've gone too far.

"Oh? You think I made an ass of myself?" she says, her voice soft and low. Too soft. Too low.

"Well, I didn't really mean that. . . ."

"Oh, I think you did."

"Glenny, why don't we just drop it?"

"If you ever call me Glenny again..." She stops. Looks at me. I look at her. She smiles. *"Did I ever tell you I still got me that baseball bat I used on Linn?"*

Once at the station, I settled down to work, trying to think of another avenue to go down to find a lead in Glenda Sue's death. Everything seemed to be dead-ended. But that was interrupted by a four-car pile up on Highway 5 that took all available personnel. I rode with Dalton, while Mike came in his car. As we neared the scene, we could all tell it was a bad one. The ambulance came up behind us, and we all got out of our respective vehicles and went to the crash scene.

One look and I knew my afternoon would be spent telling family members about their losses. We had three dead, two to the hospital in critical condition and one in serious condition, and one standing there without a scratch on him and the smell of liquor so heavy in the bright, cold morning air it was enough to gag a normal person. Ain't it always the way? One drunk caused four cars to collide, killed three people and sent three to the hospital—one a baby not more than two years old—and him without a scratch on him.

It took a couple of hours to get the county crews out to clean up the mess and notify the next of kin. One of my least favorite jobs. And I spent the afternoon interviewing the survivors, getting enough evidence to put the drunk away for as long as possible.

Now I'm a beer drinker, and, if the truth be known, I may of been behind the wheel of a car once or twice in my life when I shouldn't have been. But that was long ago. After what I've seen on this job, you couldn't get me behind the wheel when I had more than one beer. And if I ever catch my niece or nephews drinking and driving, they won't have to worry about what the law's gonna do to them 'cause there won't be much left to jail. And that's the truth.

It was a long, grueling day, and I didn't get back to the hotel until nearly six. I was up in my room changing into my evening clothes, blue jeans and a sweatshirt, when the phone rang. I picked it up, saying, "Hello?"

"Milt? Melissa. I'm down in the restaurant with Dr. McDonnell. We wondered if you'd like to bring my daughter and the rest of the crew and join us?"

"Yeah, be there in a jiffy." I changed out of the sweatshirt into a fresh white button-down, but kept on the jeans. Somebody told me once I had a cute ass for an old guy. And jeans sort of accentuate that fact. Or so I'm told. I splashed on some Aqua Velva, looked at myself in the mirror, and decided

I was a definite hunk. If of the older, pudgier variety.

I rounded up the troops and marched down to the restaurant, where Melissa had taken two tables. After kissing her baby hello, she plopped her down with the kids at one table, while us adults took the other. It was five minutes before Harmon Monk became one of us adults. And he and Jewel sat there the whole time alternately looking daggers at each other and wanting to be alone.

Dr. McDonnell was wearing a blue blouse under a winter-white suit. Businesslike in a sexy sorta way. Or sexy in a businesslike sorta way. Whichever.

Everybody talked, and she smiled a lot, her broad face breaking into dimples every time she did. I felt guilty, sitting in the restaurant where Glenda Sue worked for thirty years, staring at the dimples of another woman. Not guilty enough to stop, though.

By seven-thirty everybody was through and ready to head upstairs. I offered to walk Dr. McDonnell to her car.

"Thanks, Mr. Kovak," she said. So I did.

I've never been a fast walker, never in all that much of a hurry to get anywhere, so I had no trouble staying in step with her and her crutches. She handled them well, like a part of her body, which I guess they were by now. However long she'd had them.

By way of conversation, I said, "You're lucky to have Melissa on your team. She's gonna be a real asset."

She smiled. Dimpled like a son of a bitch. "One day and I can already tell that, Mr. Kovak." We walked for a while, then she added, "You and her mother were not married, right?"

I shook my head.

"I just wondered. When Melissa introduced you, it was as her stepfather."

"Well, just wishful thinking on both our parts. She never had a daddy. I never had a kid." I shrugged.

She smiled. And stopped. And turned towards me. "That's nice." Again, I shrugged. "You're a nice man, Mr. Kovak."

I started to walk on but noticed that she stayed where she was. "This is my car," she said, pointing to the new Chrysler she was standing in front of.

I came back. "Oh, sorry."

Dr. McDonnell laughed that light, tinkly laugh I was beginning to want to listen to for the rest of my life. "I embarrassed you."

"Not hard."

"Why?"

I shrugged. "Is why all that important?"

I had her on the run. "Can I ask you a personal question?"

She smiled and looked down at her legs. "Why the braces?"

I nodded.

"Polio. I contracted it about a year before the Salk vaccine came out."

"That's rough luck."

It was her turn to shrug, and she did it real nice. "I was five when it happened, so I really can't remember not having the braces." She grinned. "I guess it's somewhat like going bald—you get used to it."

I grinned back. "Touché," I said, leaning down and opening the driver's-side door. "Night, Dr. McDonnell."

"Good night, Mr. Kovak. And good luck tonight. No more dreams."

I smiled. "I made it last night without one," I said. "This is a new pattern I'm planning. No more dreams."

Like hell. That night it came again. The cobblestone floor, my footsteps the only sound as I walked across it, not knowing where I was going or why. All new, all unfamiliar. All old, all very familiar. I got to the escalator. Only one. Going up. I got on and the sound of my footsteps died away, replaced by nothing but silence. I saw the floor above me, then Rebecca coming into view slowly, first her feet, tiny feet clad in black patent-leather Mary Janes with white ankle socks, little brown legs and little brown knees, then the hem of her dress, a red dress made of dotted swiss, with a white bodice and collar and cuffs. Then her face and her curly hair. And she was looking down at me, her big brown eyes staring at me, sad eyes, mournful eyes. And then the legs were there, the woman legs, the sensible shoes and braces, their metal brackets going under the shoes and up the legs, disappearing under the hem of the skirt. A brown skirt. A brown wool skirt. A hand came down. Rebecca looked up, reaching up with her tiny hand, and took the hand of the woman. Looking back at me with the sad, sad eyes, she turned, following the woman away.

I stood on the escalator, moving slowly upward. Finally, I reached the top. I looked in all directions. Finally, I saw them, walking away from me, down a carpeted hall, the little girl and the tall, tall woman and her braced legs. The only sound was the shuffle of her sensible shoes on the carpeted floor. I tried to follow, but my feet wouldn't let me. I looked down. Both of my feet were stuck at the top of the escalator, the toes of my shoes being sucked into the mechanism at the top. I watched as

my feet disappeared into the machinery, then my
ankles, my calves. I looked up and saw Rebecca
and Dr. McDonnell at the end of the hall. They
both looked back sadly at me. Then they stepped
forward and fell into space. I woke up to the sound
of Rebecca's scream.

I sat up in bed, shaking all over. The sound came
again. Rebecca's scream. This time I knew it was
real, not part of any dream. I jumped out of bed
and ran out into the hall. The door to Melissa's
room was open. I ran to it and turned on the light.
Melissa lay on the floor by the bed, unmoving.
Rebecca was gone.

TEN

I RAN TO MELISSA where she lay in a shadow on the floor next to the double bed. I touched her face and my hand felt sticky. Quickly, I switched on the lamp next to the bed. Her head was bloody, and so was my hand. With my clean hand I felt her neck, looking for the carotid artery, but before I could find it, she moaned. She was alive. At least Melissa was alive. I grabbed the phone off the nightstand and called the ambulance and Emmett. Then I began looking under the bed, in the closet, in the bathroom, anywhere I could think of where Rebecca might be. But that opened door to the room told me what I didn't want to know. Rebecca was gone.

I left the room and went quickly across the hall and rapped loudly on Jewel's door. After a minute she opened it, hair mussed, holding tightly to her bathrobe. "My God, Milt, it's the middle of the..."

"Rebecca's gone. Melissa's been hurt."

I turned abruptly and headed down the hall. "Stay with Melissa till the ambulance gets here," I called over my shoulder.

I went up and down the hall, calling Rebecca's name, looking in broom closets and in stairwells. Finally, I heard the sirens and then the heavy steps on the stairs and in the halls as the emergency crews showed up to take over.

Ten minutes later I was standing on the sidewalk outside the Longbranch Inn when Emmett Hopkins said, "You need to get some clothes on."

I looked down at my T-shirt and shorts and bare feet. And noticed for the first time that the November pavement was cold to the touch. I looked again at the retreating ambulance, lights blazing, speeding towards Longbranch Memorial. The silly thought entered my head. "She's not due there for her second day for a couple of hours."

"Milt?"

I turned to Emmett. "Yeah. I'll go get dressed."

"I called Elberry. He's sending his people over here, too. We'll turn the hotel upside down for her."

"Yeah. I know."

I walked back into the hotel and took the elevator up to my room. I dressed carefully, washed the bottoms of my feet like that was an important thing to do, put on fresh underwear and a new white oxford cloth, and donned my suit pants. Then I strapped the hip holster in place, checked my .45, put it in place, and covered it with the suit coat. I was walking out the door when I remembered shoes and socks.

Once in the hallway fully dressed, I saw my niece and nephews standing in their doorways, looking at me. I walked up to Marlene and put one arm around her, opening up the other arm for the boys. All three held on to me like I was some lifeline. I didn't wanna tell 'em their lifeline was a little threadbare.

"Is Melissa gonna be all right?" Marlene asked.

It was too early in the morning, and I was too damned old to lie. I just said, "I don't know."

Leonard broke out of the huddle and headed for his room. Over his shoulder he said, "I'm getting dressed, Uncle Milt. I'll help y'all look for Rebecca."

I started to protest but decided that would take too much energy. "Okay," I said instead. Then to Marlene, I said, "Take Carl in your room, honey. Y'all stay there. Lock the door and put on the chain lock. Don't let anybody in unless it's me or your mama."

Marlene nodded and started to move Carl into her room, but nine-year-old Carl was having none of that. "I wanna help too. Uncle Milt . . ."

But I ignored him and Marlene got him into the room. It took two hours, with the help of Longbranch Inn employees, to search the hotel. It was a big place with laundry rooms, seventy-five guest rooms, conference rooms, meeting rooms, rest rooms, kitchens, auxiliary kitchens, pantries, walk-in freezer, garbage rooms, a basement, and an attic. We didn't find her. Not in attics or cellars or empty rooms or laundry carts. Rebecca was not in the hotel.

Sitting in the empty closed restaurant with cups of microwaved leftover coffee, Elberry and Emmett came to the same conclusion. "We gotta call in the FBI, Milt. It's what we gotta do," Elberry said.

I shook my head. "They won't do a goddamn thing, Elberry. Not unless we get a ransom note. At this point she's just a missing child. Local authority."

Emmett perked up. "You think maybe that's what this is? Her mama got hurt, she got scared, ran off? You think?"

"No, I don't goddamn think that!" I shouted. "Somebody snatched her. Just like somebody slit her grandma's throat. Just like somebody threw her in the storm cellar! If she'd been scared, she'da come to me!"

"Milt," Elberry said, touching my shoulder lightly.

"Uncle Milt! Uncle Milt!" We all looked up at the shouting coming from the hotel entrance to the restaurant. Marlene and Carl came bounding up, and I stood up, ready to take my wrath out on them.

"I told you to stay in your room! What in the hell..."

Marlene held out an envelope. "Somebody slipped this under our door," she said.

The front of the envelope had my name in block letters. I tore it open, read it, and turned to Elberry. "Now call the FBI," I said.

Everybody peered over my shoulder, reading what was already etched into my brain:

YOU WANT THE LITTLE MONGRAL BICH BACK YOU DO LIKE WE SAY YOU FIND WHAT THE OLE BICH TOOK AND YOU GIVE IT BACK OR THE LITTLE NIGGER GETS LIKE HER GRAMA THIS IS NO JOKE FIND IT NOW OR GET HER BACK IN PEECES

The restaurant was crowded now. Everybody reading the note. So many hands on it, fingerprints were a joke. Marlene started crying, Carl right behind her. I saw Jasmine Bodine standing behind Dalton.

"Jasmine."

She moved around Dalton, coming up to me.

"Yeah, Milt?"

"Take the kids back up to Jewel's room and stay with 'em. You don't let anybody in 'cept me or their mama. You got that?"

"Got it, Milt."

She moved the sniffling kids out of the restaurant and into the hotel. I saw Elberry over by the counter on the phone and was pretty sure I knew who he was talking to. Long-distance to Oklahoma City. The nearest FBI office.

I walked over to the counter and stood, half listening, half dead. My hands played with the items on the countertop, a display case of Lifesavers, a rack holding applications for an American Express card, and another rack holding pamphlets. I looked down at the pamphlets. "The Mongrelization of America" it said in capital letters. Down at the bottom there was a stamp. Saying, "Brought to You by the Patriots for a Free America."

I picked it up, began to read. Finding phrases like "nigger bucks impregnating white girls," "mandatory abortions for any white woman carrying a black seed," "mandatory death penalty for any nigger raping or otherwise seducing a white woman." The phrase from the note, emblazened on my brain, came back: "Mongrel bitch." My Rebecca.

I grabbed the phone book from under the counter and looked up Davey Guy's address. Elberry was still talking to the FBI. Emmett was deploying his men. Dalton was standing around with his thumb up his ass. Nobody saw me leave.

"Glenda Sue," I said out loud, "they got your grandbaby."

"You'll take care of it, Milt," she says. "You always do."

"What if I can't this time, Glenda Sue? What if I can't?"

She smiles. Touches my face. "You can do it. Shit, I've always known you can do just about anything. Except maybe make a decent cup of coffee."

Davey Guy lived in a tract house on the outskirts of Longbranch. In the county. My territory. It was a little after four in the morning when I pulled my '55 into the yard of Davey Guy's house, parking behind a fifteen-year-old El Camino. The yard was littered with motorcycles and a bass boat, car parts, and tires. The front porch held an old sofa and an even older washing machine. I rapped on the door hard. And often.

Guy finally opened the door, rubbing sleep from his eyes. He was wearing blue jeans he'd obviously just pulled on because the top button wasn't done, and no shirt. His skinny chest sprouted four lonely hairs.

"What?" he said, peering at me. "Deputy Kovak? That right?"

"Yeah, that's right," I said, pushing past him and into the living room. Kid's toys littered the floor and the smell of old urine was strong.

"Hey! What the hell!" Davey Guy glared at me. "You got a warrant?"

I pulled my gun out of my holster, grabbed the four hairs on his chest, and pushed him up against the wall, sticking the barrel of the .45 against his nose.

"Yeah. This is my warrant. My personal goddamn warrant."

"What the shit! Hey, man! Hey!"

"Where's my granddaughter?"

"What? Man, I . . ." He was shaking his head back and forth, sweat popping off his forehead, spittle dripping off his chin.

"Rebecca Robinson. The little *mongrel bitch!* Where is she?" I stuck the barrel of the gun up one nostril.

"Man! I dunno what you're talking about! Swear to God, man!"

I heard a woman scream and looked around. Davey Guy's wife was standing in the hall leading to what I presumed were bedrooms.

"Go on back," I told her. "This is between me and him."

"I'll call the cops!" she screamed, holding a flimsy housecoat across her baby-swollen belly.

"Honey, I *am* the cops! Now get!"

She scurried out of the room, and I threw Davey Guy down on the stained couch. I tossed the pamphlet at him. "This yours?" I asked.

He looked at the pamphlet. "I...uh..."

I shoved the gun back at his nose. "Is this piece of filth yours, you asshole! Answer me!"

"We get it from the National Affiliate. All this stuff. Pamphlets and stuff. We just stamp 'em and send 'em out."

"You ever read 'em, huh? Don't know what you're stamping your name to?"

"Ah...well..."

"You read this shit? *Can* you read?"

Guy bristled, getting a little of his macho back. "Yeah, man, I can read! I graduated high school! Shit!"

"What does this say?" I demanded.

"'The Mongrelization of America,'" he read.

"What does that mean?"

Davey Guy shrugged. "You know, man. Niggers and whites having babies. Like mongrel dogs. Get it?"

He was explaining it to me. He really was. "So that's bad?" I asked.

"Oh, yeah, man. Real bad. Makes 'em stupid. The babies. Nigger blood, man, you mix that with white and it makes 'em stupider than niggers even."

I pressed the gun up against his face again. "Well, your mama must have been black, 'cause you're the stupidest asshole I've ever met!"

He pushed up against me. "Hey, man! My mama wasn't no nigger! Who told you that?"

I pushed him back down with my free hand. "Shut your stupid face." I sat down opposite him on a ratty ottoman, pointing the gun at his crotch. "Somebody kidnapped a little girl tonight. A very smart little girl. My granddaughter. Her mama's white and her daddy's black. And somebody stole her. And they wrote a note calling her a mongrel bitch." I said all this real slow so it could sink in. "Now I figure it has something to do with your little organization of racist assholes. And whoever stole her had something to do with her grandma's murder. Glenda Sue Robinson? Waitress at the Longbranch? Got her throat cut? Maybe you remember some of this?"

Davey Guy had been backing up during my little speech. As far as a guy can back up when he's sitting on a couch. His butt was almost on the headrest. "Hey, man, we didn't have nothing to do with those things! Swear to God! Swear on my kids' heads, man!"

Then I remembered something. Something I'd heard at the meeting at the Longbranch Inn. "That $10,000. That anonymous contribution. Where'd it come from?"

"Huh?"

This guy was so stupid I felt like shooting him just so he couldn't breed anymore. "At your last meeting. Your treasurer read the financial report. There was a $10,000 anonymous contribution. Where'd it come from?"

"Oh, that. I dunno."

"You don't know?"

"No, man, I don't know! That's what anonymous means!"

"Who would know?"

"Huh?"

"Would Marty Vanderhoff know who gave y'all that money?"

"Ah, well . . . I guess. I dunno. Maybe."

"And they made you president."

"Huh?"

I holstered the .45, got up, and walked out.

ELEVEN

I'D PULLED MY '55 up next to the phone booth in the parking lot of the Quick Mart and was looking through the phone book for Marty Vanderhoff's address when the sheriff found me.

He got out of the car and walked up to the booth, leaning against it. "Well, hello, there," he said.

"Hi," I said, waiting for the other shoe to drop.

"You've been a busy little fella, now haven't you?"

"Cut to the chase, Elberry. I'm not in a game-playing mood."

"Now that's not what Lolly May Guy said when she called the office, complaining that one of my men was playing games with her husband. Shoving a gun up his nose is what I heard."

"The FBI show up yet?"

He shook his head. "Takes them fellas a while. Probably be noon or so."

"She could be dead by then."

"Son . . ."

"Don't 'son' me, Elberry! Just go away. I got work to do."

"Boy..." he slammed the phone book closed on my hand. "You're too close to this. Back off for a while. Give me that gun and your badge, and you just back off."

I pulled my gun out of my holster and stuck it in his ample gut. "This the gun you want, sheriff?"

"I'm gonna forget you done that, Milton. Now hand it over."

"Get out of my way." I shoved the gun deeper into his gut for emphasis. He backed away, allowing me to get out of the claustrophobic phone booth. "Now I got things to do. I'm following up on a lead. You got a lead? No, you don't. I got a lead. And I'm following up on it. You understand that, sheriff? I'm following up on a lead that's gonna get me to Rebecca. While she's maybe still in one piece. You understand that?"

I was just about finished with my speech when I felt something stick me in the back. Then I heard Mike Neils say, "Milton, now put that gun down. Hand it to the sheriff real slowlike. Okay, Milton, you do that, okay?"

I handed the gun to Elberry Blankenship. He unloaded it and threw the .45 through the open window of his car. "Mike, you didn't see nothing here, you understand?" the sheriff said.

"Yes, sir."

"Go on now."

We waited, Elberry and me, staring at each other, as Mike Neils got back in his car and drove off.

"Go on to the hospital and check on Melissa. Or go back to the hotel and check on the kids. This is his case. He just called me in for manpower. I was happy to oblige. But I name the men who's working this, and I ain't naming you. You understand?"

I turned and got into my '55 and drove off. I'd managed to get Marty Vanderhoff's address before the sheriff had closed the book, and I drove over there. He lived in town, in one of the post-war houses that sprang up in the early fifties. Neat and trim it was, too. But nobody was home. I figured while the Guys were doing some calling, they must have called Marty, too.

Two blocks from Marty Vanderhoff's house, I passed a mailbox that said, "McDonnell." There were empty boxes next to the curb, waiting for trash pickup, like somebody's just moved in. The car in the driveway, the same new Chrysler I'd seen the night before, had a handicapped license plate. The memory of my dream came back to me. Rebecca and the lady with the legs. Dr. McDonnell. I parked next to the curb and got out. It was after five in the morning. Not much after, but some. I walked up the sidewalk to the front porch and rang the bell. Then rang it again. I heard someone moving around inside and stood there, waiting.

She was wearing a flannel bathrobe. Red plaid. Her hair was mussed, and she wasn't wearing any makeup. Her feet were bare, without sensible shoes or braces. She stood there leaning on her crutches. "Mr. Kovak?"

I pushed past her into the house. The living room was the kind of mess you'd expect from someone who'd just moved in. The furniture was nice, expensive stuff. Paintings leaned against appropriate walls, not yet hung. Boxes of books sat by built-in bookcases next to the fireplace. The kitchen, which opened into the living room, had boxes on all the counters.

Still by the door, I heard Dr. McDonnell say, "What is it you want, Deputy?"

"I wanna know what you had to do with all this," I said, turning to her.

She frowned. "All what?"

"I keep dreaming about you . . . now all of you, not just your legs. I keep dreaming about you taking Rebecca, and now she's gone. So I wanna know what you know about all of this."

"Rebecca's gone? Where? What do you mean?"

I moved towards her, put my hands on her arms, squeezing hard. "Tell me! I gotta know!"

She pulled away, almost losing her balance. "Sit down," she said. "Would you like some coffee? It'll just take a minute."

I nodded and sat while she went into the kitchen, busying herself with the coffee. In a minute she was back out, sitting down on the couch next to me. "What happened?" she asked.

I leaned my head back against the couch, staring at the ceiling. At the old-fashioned light fixture that hung there. "I heard Rebecca scream. First in the dream. Then I woke up and she was still screaming. I ran out in the hall. The door to their room was open. Melissa was lying on the floor, her head all bloody. Rebecca was gone. Melissa . . . Melissa's unconscious. They took her to the hospital. We got a note . . . about Rebecca."

And I told her what it had said.

She touched her hand to my cheek. Her long fingers tracing my brow.

"I don't know why you're dreaming about me, about me hurting Rebecca. Milt, I'm sorry."

Before I knew what I was doing, my mouth was on hers, everything in my head being blown away and leaving nothing behind except the need. The god-awful need to have this woman, to block out the hurt and the pain. To stop thinking and only feel. Her long fingers tugged at my belt, my jacket slid off my shoulders. I removed my holster, laying the rig down on the coffee table, laying her down on the couch.

An hour and a half later she came out of the bedroom, braces on her legs, clothes on her body. She came up behind me, ruffling my hair with those fingers. I shook my head.

"What?" she said.

"You shoulda told me."

"Told you what?"

"You know."

She laughed, the fingers playing through my hair. "You mean, 'Oh, by the way, Milton, you're about to deflower a forty-four-year-old virgin. I hope you don't mind.'"

"Why?"

"Why was I a virgin, or why did I make love to you?"

"Both."

She came around and sat down beside me, taking my hand in hers and playing with my nails. Not looking at me, her voice soft, she said, "I guess nobody ever needed me quite that much." Again she laughed, her blue eyes finding mine and holding them. "When you're in the field I'm in, you find out that most psychiatrists are crazier than their patients."

"I don't know what to say," I said.

"How about thank you?"

I looked at her and she laughed again. That tinkling, musical laugh. "Well, you're acting like it's some gigantic thing. So be properly grateful."

"Thank you," I said.

"Your welcome," she said. "Anytime."

I looked at her, the smooth, velvety skin, the green-blue eyes, the dimples when she smiled. "Any time?" I asked.

She put her arms around my neck and leaned her breasts against me. "Except when I have a patient in the office. That could be awkward. Not impossible, mind you, just awkward."

"For a recently deflowered virgin, you are one ribald lady."

"Think about it this way. Can you imagine what would happen if Hoover Dam ever burst?"

I grinned. "Doesn't bear thinking about."

She stood up and pulled me with her. "Drive me to the hospital," she said. "Let's check on Melissa."

It was still early, before the hospital started waking up with breakfast trays and morning meds. Because I was with Dr. McDonnell (who's first name I didn't even know yet), we had no trouble getting in to see Melissa.

She was awake and sitting up, a white bandage around her head, Jewel in the chair by her side.

"Have you found her?" she demanded.

"No, honey, not yet." I sat down on the bed beside her. "But the FBI's coming in on it."

"The FBI? I don't understand. . . ."

"There was a ransom note." I told her what it said, sorta. Leaving out the nasty stuff.

"Oh, God, Mama!" Melissa said, tears rolling down her face. "What the hell have you done?"

"Can you think of anyplace Glenda Sue mighta hid something? Anyplace at all?"

Melissa gingerly shook her head. "The trailer. The car."

"No, we've checked both."

"At the restaurant?"

"We checked there, too." I told her about the ticket we found.

She leaned her head back against the pillow. "I'm sorry, Milt," she said. I didn't say anything.

The silence was broken by Dr. McDonnell, who turned to Jewel. "Why don't I buy you a cup of coffee? That way Milt and Melissa can talk more freely."

Jewel looked at her. "That sounds fine. Except I don't know who you are."

"Jean McDonnell. Melissa's boss."

The two left with me looking after. Jean. Like Gene Tierney, Jean Arthur. Good name, Jean.

"Are they going to kill my baby?"

I looked back to the bed, to the head in its white bandages leaning against the white pillows. How do you answer a question like that? "Not if I can help it."

"What can you do?"

"Find them. Find whatever it is Glenda Sue hid. Money probably. She had to have money to buy that plane ticket. Money to think she could just take off, give up her job." I stopped and thought. "Where would she have gotten it? The money?"

Melissa closed her eyes. "I don't know. You knew her better than I did, really. Knew what her life was like the last few years." The eyes opened and she looked at me. "Where would she have gotten the money?"

I glanced out the window at the heavily overcast sky. The temperature was forty-two degrees. Fifty percent chance of rain. I hoped wherever Rebecca was, it was indoors. "She found it. Nobody'd give it to her. For safekeeping, something like that. I don't think anybody'd do that. Not this much money. It has to be a lot. For her to think . . ."

Melissa touched my hand. "This must have hurt you, Milt. To know she was running off. How do you feel about that?"

I smiled and turned my hand over to grasp hers. "Don't play shrink with me today, honey. Later, maybe."

Melissa laughed ruefully. "Habit."

"Where? Where would she get it? Where would she hide it?" I mused.

"The Longbranch Inn," Melissa said.

I looked at her. "Which?"

"Where she got it. Where else did she go? The trailer or the Longbranch. Am I right?"

I nodded. "Yeah, you're right. That's about all she did. Unless she was with me. I think I woulda noticed her picking up a bundle of money someplace."

"Then she got it at the Longbranch."

"What? Somebody left behind a briefcase full of cash? At one of the tables? Maybe somebody in one of the rooms?"

Slowly she shook her head. "I don't know. I'm just..."

Then she began to cry, great heaving sobs that shook her body. All I could do was hold her, pat her, wait for it all to go away.

TWELVE

I HEADED BACK to the Longbranch Inn, stopping by Marty Vanderhoff's on the way. Still nobody at home. The sun had decided to peek out of the clouds for a minute, the minute I was parked in Marty Vanderhoff's driveway. If it hadn't decided to do that, I may not have noticed the reflection coming off something inside the garage. I got out of the car and went and peered in one of the little windows that ran across the front of the garage door.

Inside were two cars. A four-year-old Olds Ninety-eight and a brand new Toyota pickup. Two cars were curious. One car would have led to the assumption that Marty and his wife had left in the other. Most people nowadays have two. If there's two drivers in the family. Three if there's three. A used-car parking lot if there's more. Some houses in Longbranch with teenagers have cars in the garage, the driveway, and sitting in the middle of the yard. Not an uncommon sight.

But I knew Marty Vanderhoff didn't have teenagers. In fact, I knew he didn't have any kids at all. I saw the notice not six months back in the church bulletin that nuptials were to be said for Robin Camp, a member of the church, and Marty Vanderhoff. Robin worked checkout at the Foodworld. The Foodworld was too far away for them to have walked. I went back to the front door of the house and knocked again. And again. Still no answer.

I walked around to the back of the house, going through a little gate that separated the backyard and back door from the driveway and garage. The backyard was well kept. With neatly coiled hoses snug up against the wall of the house, a barbecue pit all shiny and new, leaves recently raked. I walked up the little stoop to the back door and knocked. No answer. I tried the door, but it was locked. Then I shielded my eyes from the glare of the day and peered through the window, trying to get a look through a little split in the curtains. All I could see was the utility room, all neat and clean.

I went down the stairs of the stoop and turned, looking at the back of the house. There was a window a few feet from the back door that probably looked into the kitchen, covered in miniblinds with the slats turned vertical. But it was a good six feet off the ground. Me being five foot ten and half, I didn't think I could see too well through it.

Behind the garage I found a produce crate big enough to give me the boost up I needed. I hauled it over to the window and stood on it. Shielding my eyes again, I looked into the kitchen. And saw the newlyweds sitting down to breakfast. Except there was blood in the cornflakes and brain tissue in the Cream of Wheat.

I jumped down off the crate and went to the '55 to call it in. Twenty minutes later I was sitting in Emmett Hopkins's office being grilled by him, the sheriff looking on as he stood propped up by the door.

"So how come you went by there anyways?" Emmett asked.

"I thought Marty might know something about Rebecca being missing," I answered.

"Milt, you shoot them two?"

I sighed. "Elberry took my gun early this morning. Ask him. I don't have another."

"What about them six-shooters?"

"Jesus, Emmett, give me a break!"

"What made you think Marty Vanderhoff had anything to do with Rebecca's kidnapping?"

So I told him. About the Patriots of a Free America, their propaganda, all of it.

"Now wait just a goddamn minute," Elberry said. "I know them guys. They ain't like that."

"The hell they ain't!" I said, looking at my boss square in the eye. I reached into my inside coat pocket and brought out the pamphlet that still rested there. "Read this shit."

Elberry read a little and threw the brochure on Emmett's desk. "That's just talk. Has nothing to do with this here."

I told them both about the mysterious $10,000 donation. And Davey Guy saying as how Marty Vanderhoff would be the one to ask who the donation had come from. "And now Marty Vanderhoff's dead. Now there's no way to find out who the donation came from. Real convenient, huh?" I said.

Elberry came up behind me and put his hand heavily on my shoulder. "You're too close to this, Milt. You're seeing things. Imagining things...."

Emmett leaned back in his chair and said, "I don't know, Elberry. I'm seeing some sort of connection here myself."

Elberry removed his hand from my shoulder and marched towards the door. "I ain't gonna be a party to rousting honest citizens. You do what you think best, Emmett." And he left.

Emmett and I both looked out the glass walls at Elberry Blankenship's retreating back. "Now what the hell was that all about?" Emmett said.

I shook my head. "I don't know. But you with me on this?"

Emmett swiveled halfway in his chair, back and forth, then looked at me. "I'm interested. Maybe..."

"You're in or you're out, Emmett. And it's gotta be now."

He picked up the Patriots for a Free America pamphlet that rested on his desk and began reading. Finally, with a shake of his head and a disgusted look on his face, he said, "Shit. Come on."

We got in Emmett's squad car and headed for the Longbranch. I went first up to Jewel's room on the fourth floor. All three kids were there, Marlene and Carl still huddled in their nightclothes, with Jasmine Bodine watching them.

It was getting close to schooltime. "Jasmine, you stay with Marlene while she gets ready, and I'll go with the boys. Then would you mind taking 'em all to school and warning the principal? Keep an eye out."

"Sure, Milt. No problem," she said, sighing her heavy sigh that was nothing more than a characteristic of being a Nail girl. For a while, right after she left Lester Bodine, Jasmine had perked up some. But her born sad nature had been returning for a while now.

I oversaw the boys getting ready and then left the three of 'em in Jasmine's care, heading on back downstairs where Emmett waited for me in the restaurant, having his umpteenth cup of coffee of the morning.

"So now what?" he asked as I sat down, signaling to Loretta Dubchek for coffee.

"I don't know. I been thinking ... Glenda Sue worked here for thirty years. That's all she did. Work here. The Patriots for a Free America have their meetings here. There's racks of their garbage over there by the cash register.... I'm just thinking...."

"What? What are you thinking?" Emmett asked, getting a little impatient.

"Seems to be one thing connecting all these things together. And it's the Longbranch Inn. And the Longbranch Inn is Maynard Dabney. Plain and simple."

Emmett took a long sip of his coffee, then looked me in the eye. "Thing to do right now, as I see it," he said, "is go have us a chat with Mr. Dabney."

We both stood up, left coins on the table for our coffees, and headed to the back of the building where Maynard Dabney's office was. Walking in unannounced, we startled Elberry Blankenship sitting at a chair in front of Maynard's desk. I was a little startled myself.

Elberry and Maynard both stood up. Elberry said, "What you two up to now?"

Emmett nodded. This was his call, and I let him lead the way. "Elberry, Maynard. Turning out to be a pretty day," he said, glancing out the window at the sun now shining brightly. The fifty percent chance of rain seeming like somebody's idea of a joke.

"Yeah, it is at that," the sheriff said.

"Maynard, you got a minute?" Emmett said.

"Sure, Chief, sit on down."

Everybody sat. Maynard in his chair behind the desk, Elberry in the one he'd just vacated, and Emmett in the one that was left. Rank had me leaning up against the door jamb.

"Wanted to ask you a few questions if I could," Emmett started.

"Anybody want some coffee? All I gotta do is call Loretta. She'd be glad to bring a pot."

"Thank you, but I'm all coffeed out." Glancing back at me, Emmett said, "How 'bout you, Milt?" I shook my head. Looking at Maynard again, Emmett smiled. "We're fine, thank you," he said.

I looked on with admiration. I hadn't seen Emmett work in a while. The man was good.

"Now, Maynard, what I wanted to ask you about is this group that meets here. The Patriots of a Free America. Marty Vanderhoff was their treasurer, I understand."

Maynard shook his head. "I wouldn't know anything about that. That's a public room they rent. They got the money to pay for it, they get the room."

"So you'd just let any old body meet there, huh?" Emmett asked, his voice sounding genuinely puzzled. "The American Legion, the Garden Club, the Communist party?"

Maynard laughed. "We ain't got no Communists in Prophesy County, right, Elberry?"

Elberry didn't laugh. Actually, he didn't do much of anything. Just sat there.

"So you don't know nothing about this group, huh?" Emmett asked again.

"I already told you that. No, I don't."

"Then how come you let them put their brochures by the cash register?"

"It was part of the deal."

"Oh, I see," Emmett said, leaning back in his chair, the front two legs coming off the floor as he stretched his legs out. "You rent the room. You also rent that little space by the cash register."

Maynard didn't say anything. Emmett's chair legs came down with a crash so loud even I jumped, and I was expecting it. "That's bullshit, Maynard," Emmett said, his voice soft. "What do you think I'd find if I got me a list of all the members of the Patriots for a Free America?" he asked, saying the name of the group like it was a bad taste in his mouth.

"I don't know, Emmett, why don't you tell me?"

"Think I'd find your name on that list?"

Maynard laughed. "Not hardly!" Maynard leaned forward across his desk top. "Look, Chief, I don't got nothing to do with them people. They rent the room. That's all. Now I got work to do here. I got a business to run. You got any more questions?"

Emmett stood up. "Not right now. But I'll be back."

He turned and walked to the door, which I had opened for him. Glancing over my shoulder, I saw Elberry Blankenship looking at me. And if looks could kill, I'd be in heaven with the angels.

"Where to now?" I asked as Emmett and I got back in his car.

"Well, I'd surely like to have me a talk with ol' Davey Guy. But that's not my jurisdiction."

"It's mine," I said.

"Elberry took your shield."

"What makes you think that?"

Emmett looked at me. He started the engine. "My mistake," he said, pulling out and heading out of town.

The door to Davey Guy's house stood open. The El Camino, the bass boat, and the motorcycle were gone, and the house was empty of everything but trash. Looked like the Guy family had skipped.

Emmett and I piled through the trash, finding nothing worth our efforts, then got back in the car. Starting the engine, Emmett asked, "You remember anybody else at that meeting besides Guy and Vanderhoff?"

"Well, they had a speaker, but he wasn't local. Name of Chester Oliver."

"Any locals you can think of?"

"Not members. I didn't notice any of them. But one guy sitting in the back with me, a newcomer, was good ol' Lester Bodine."

Emmett snorted. "Sounds like the kind of organization Lester would be prone to."

"Don't it, though?"

It was now past nine in the morning. Rebecca had been missing for five hours. Jean's image kept popping up and I shoved that back down. No time to think of that either. Tried to concentrate on what I was gonna say to Lester Bodine as Emmett parked in the parking lot of Bodine's Food and Grain.

Earl Bodine, Lester's daddy, stood behind the counter when we entered. We were back on city ground, so Emmett took over.

"Morning, Earl," he said, extending his hand.

"Morning, Emmett. Milt. How you doing? Sorry to hear about Glenda Sue," he said, shaking Emmett's hand then mine.

"Thanks," I said, staying behind Emmett, letting him lead the way.

"Lester around?" the chief of police asked.

Earl frowned. "What's this about, Emmett?"

"Just need to ask him some questions, Earl. Think he might be a witness to something is all. He around?"

Earl motioned with his shoulder to the back door of the small store. "Out back loading feed." His frown deepened. "Everything okay?"

Emmett smiled. "Everything's just fine, Earl. Don't you worry."

I hadn't seen Lester Bodine to talk to since the night his wife, my deputy, Jasmine, hacked off his foreskin with a steak knife. What you might call the official beginning of their separation. He was looking a whole lot better than he had at that time.

"Hey, Chief, Milt," Lester called from his perch high atop a stack of feed sacks. "Can I help you?"

"Sure can, Lester. Come on down here a minute," Emmett said.

Lester scrambled down, wiped his hands on his pants legs and shook hands with both of us. "How's Jasmine?" he asked me.

I smiled. "Just fine," I said.

He nodded his head, the look on his face plainly saying that's not what he wanted to hear. I suppose he wanted me to say she cried all day at the station, wailing away for her lost Lester or some such shit.

"Lester," Emmett said, leaning against a stack of feed sacks, "Milton here says he saw you last week at that meeting of them Patriots for a Free America."

Lester nodded. "Yeah. I didn't see you there, Milt."

"I was way in the back."

"What can you tell me about that group, Lester?" Emmett asked.

Lester shrugged. "Not much. I just went with some guys from the Sidewinder," he said, naming our little hellhole of fame out on Highway 5, our one and only honky-tonk. "They was a little too political for my taste. Like I said, I was just along for the ride."

"You know anybody who's a member?" I asked.

Again he shrugged. "Yeah. Davey Guy's the president. And Bob Renfroe's the . . . something . . . what they call that? . . . Sergeant at arms? Something like that."

"Anybody else?"

Slowly, he listed three more names. Members, not officers. John Ashbaugh, Curtis Allen, and Mickey Loomis. We thanked him and headed back to Emmett's car.

"Bobby Leroi Renfroe. Sergeant at Arms," Emmett said. "At least they got them some bulk for the job."

I nodded. Remembering Bobby Leroi. Remembering him well. He broke my nose and dislocated my collarbone while I managed to read him his rights. All in the line of duty. One of those Saturday nights at the Sidewinder. Bobby with too much booze and too little restraint, trying to dissuade a fella from flirting with his lady of the moment. It was my own damned fault, the broken nose and dislocated collarbone. I should have gone in with a bazooka.

Bobby Leroi Renfroe was the biggest and best fullback the Longbranch Cougars ever had. One mean son of a bitch. Missed a scholarship to OU simply because he was in jail at the time they were giving 'em out. And now here was Emmett driving to his house. Oh, boy.

Bobby still lived with his mama in a big ole tumbling down two-story about a block from downtown. We pulled into the driveway and got out, walking gingerly up the rotting porch steps and knocking on the door frame of the house, afraid to knock on the door lest it fall down.

Mrs. Renfroe answered the door, her dyed red hair still in curlers and her exceptionally nice body for a lady her age clad in skin-tight jeans and an off-the-shoulder sweater.

"Miz Renfroe," Emmett said, tipping his hat and smiling. "How are you this morning?"

She squinted at him through the smoke that curled past her eyes from the cigarette dangling out of the center of her red red mouth. Almost made me wanna quit smoking. Almost. "Chief? What you want? Bobby's been here all morning asleep. And all night last night. He didn't do nothing."

"No, ma'am, it's nothing like that. I just need to ask him a few questions. He's not in any trouble."

Esther Renfroe wasn't buying that. There'd been hardly a day in her son's life when he hadn't been. In trouble, that is.

"Well, he's sleeping. Don't wanna wake him up."

"Well, I understand that, ma'am. But it's real important that we talk to him. I'd much rather do it here in your presence than haul him down to the station."

Mrs. Renfroe opened the door and ushered us into the parlor of the house that had belonged to the Renfroe family for longer than anybody could remember. Some of the furniture in the parlor looked like it had come over on covered wagons with the first Renfroes, except now the wood tops were marred with white circles from ill-placed drinks, ashtrays overloaded, and cigarette burns on the good wood. Mrs. Renfroe picked up her glass from beside the chair where she'd been sitting. It looked like orange juice, but the smell of her breath said the orange juice had a bit of nip to it.

"Y'all just wait here. I'll go get Bobby."

Emmett and I stood looking around the room. Pictures of old Renfroes glared down from the halls, sternly telling us things weren't going as well for the family as they had originally planned. After about five minutes, we heard a car start up in the driveway. Emmett looked at me, and I looked at him, and we hightailed it out the door, me with Esther Renfroe holding on to my suit coat, yelling, "Let him go! He didn't do nothing!"

Since we'd parked in the driveway, we had Bobby Leroi blocked, but he was trying his best to move Emmett's car by crashing into it again and again. It was working, too. The city squad car was slowly moving backwards down the long driveway. Not so much rolling, since the brake was on, but sorta scooching.

Emmett pulled his gun, and I just sorta stood there, since I didn't have a gun to pull. He grabbed the door handle of Bobby's car and jerked, opening it and grabbing Bobby by the scruff of the neck. I moved in and helped him haul the last of the Renfroes out of his car. Bobby Leroi was flailing away, hitting Emmett a good punch in the ribs and me in the ear before we had him down on the ground, arms behind him, hands cuffed. Esther Renfroe stood on the front porch yelling at us.

We got Bobby up and put him in the back of the squad car and drove slowly back to the station, listening to the front fender of the car squeal against the grill with each jolt.

THIRTEEN

After Emmett had read Bobby Leroi his rights and slammed him into a cell to cool off, we went to Emmett's office, where he got a manual out of his desk drawer.

"What you doing?" I asked.

"Getting ready to swear you in as a temporary auxiliary police officer. I can do that."

"Oh," I said and raised my right hand as instructed and instantly went on the payroll of the Longbranch city government. Temporarily.

"I figure we can do this since Elberry suspended you. You're not double-dipping. But I need you to have a little firepower." He went to the gun rack on the back wall of his office and took a key out of his pocket, fitted it into the keyhole, and opened the door. "Name your poison."

I went over and looked at the rack of guns: 45s, shotguns, sniper rifles, etc., etc. I picked an ugly .45 that looked and felt a lot like the one Elberry had taken away from me. I figured it best to stick with what was familiar.

"I don't know what we're getting into here, Milt," Emmett said, "but I think it best we're both armed to the teeth.'' He brought out a double bar-reled 12-gauge sawed-off. Emmett opened the drawer beneath the rack for ammo. Selecting a supply to hold me over for an evasion of any size, I felt a little like Rambo going off to battle. Just a little. Didn't have no ammo belts, though, to criss-cross my manly chest.

Emmett laid his arsenal on his desk top and said, ''I think we've given Bobby Leroi time enough to cool down. Let's me and you go have a little chat with him.''

One of Emmett's officers set Bobby Leroi up for us in a little conference room. We went in and had a seat. First thing out of the boy's mouth was, ''Anybody got a cigarette?''

I shook a Marlboro out of my pack and got a wide-eyed stare from Emmett. I lit up with Bobby and we sat there silently smoking and staring at each other a minute.

''I know you?'' Bobby Leroi finally asked, poking his cigarette in my direction.

''Yeah. I arrested you once. Over at the Side-winder.'' His face lit up all smiles.

''Yeah, man, I remember that. Busted you up good, too!'' He laughed like an idiot.

''So tell us what you did with the little girl,'' I said, taking on the bad guy even though Emmett had given me the good guy role while we were out in the hall. The asshole's attitude was pushing me in the wrong direction. I figured Emmett could just wing it.

"What little girl?" he said, leaning back in his chair and studying the ceiling.

"The little girl you helped kidnap from the Longbranch Inn," I said, leaning forward and smiling my meanest smile. I got one of those. Got a whole bagful of meaningful smiles used just for interrogation.

"Man, I don't know what you're talking about." He blew smoke towards the ceiling, and I stood up, leaned across the table, and knocked him upside the head hard as I could. The Marlboro flew out of his hand and landed on the floor. He caught himself from falling out of the chair. Bobby Leroi stood up sharply like he was coming for me, and Emmett showed him his gun.

"Sit back down, Bobby Leroi," he said calmly. To me he said, "Milton, you shouldn't oughta do that."

I was shaking all over, and most of it wasn't playacting. "Just let me kill him now, Emmett. We can find out what we need some other place."

"No, now, Milton, I don't know if Bobby Leroi's as mixed up in this as you think he is. We know the money came from the Longbranch, and it had something to do with that Patriot bunch of his, and maybe they're the ones who kidnapped the little girl, but I think if Bobby Leroi knows anything about this, it's just nothing but an accident. Am I right, Bobby?''

I was watching the last of the Renfroes while Emmett made his little speech. At the mention of the money, his face went pale, the color coming back a little when he saw his out.

''I mighta heard something,'' he ventured, leaning forward in his chair.

''Well, that could be helpful, Bobby Leroi,'' Emmett said, smiling. ''What might you have heard?''

''I dunno. Something about...maybe somebody thinking they could ransomlike the nigger kid for the money.'' He sat up straighter. ''Which I don't know nothing about. The money.''

''Where you think they might be keeping the little girl, Bobby?''

''Hey, man, if I knew that I'd have to be in on it, wouldn't I? What you think, I'm stupid or something?''

I felt Emmett's hand on my leg, holding me down. He said, ''Now seems to me you coulda overheard someone talking about it. That you knowing where the kid is could be real innocent.''

Bobby Leroi looked up at the ceiling again. Finally, looking back at Emmett, he smiled and said,

"Man, I don't know jack shit. Except I think it's time I got me a lawyer. And I ain't saying another word till I see him. Understand?"

Emmett turned Bobby Leroi over to one of his officers, who led him to a phone for his call, then Emmett and I went back to his office, where the fibbie was waiting. There was no doubt, walking in, that the man sitting behind Emmett's desk was FBI. No doubt in the world. One, we were expecting him, and two, nobody dresses as nondescript as the FBI. Generic suits.

He stood and shook hands with Emmett. "Chief Hopkins?" he asked.

Emmett smiled and nodded. "That's right."

"Michael Donnelley, Federal Bureau of Investigation."

"Fine. Glad you got here." Emmett gracefully ushered Donnelley into one of the visitor's chairs and took his own chair back. I sat down in the other. "This here," he said, pointing at me, "is Chief Deputy Kovak of the Sheriff's Department, on loan to me on this case."

Donnelley and I shook hands.

"The missing child," Emmett went on, "is Deputy Kovak's granddaughter."

Donnelley cleared his throat. "Well, now, Chief, that isn't exactly procedural. Having a family member..."

"He's a sworn officer of the law, Agent Donnelley, and he knows this case better than anybody else."

From there, Donnelley sat quietly while Emmett and I filled him in. I finished with, "They call themselves Patriots for a Free America, and the president said they got their propaganda bullshit from their national office. You ever hear of 'em?"

"No, and I'm pretty up on the white supremacists now operating. You have one of their brochures?"

I pulled the crumpled piece of paper out of my pocket and handed it to him. Donnelley read it for a minute then said, "Shit."

We both looked at him.

"Sorry," he said, clearing his throat. I suppose fibbies aren't allowed to curse. No wonder they're all so goddamn uptight. He waved the pamphlet at us. "The mongrelization stuff... it's kind of a trademark of the United Aryan Brethren. This is one of their pamphlets; I'd recognize it anywhere. We locked up most of the big boys in that group about six years ago. All except the top dog. Andrew J. Minike. Far as we know, he left the country. But these guys were into everything. Gun running, armored car heists, you name it, these guys were into it. In a serious way. But we thought the rest of them had scattered. But now I'm not so sure."

"You know a guy named Chester Oliver?" I asked, remembering the speaker at the meeting I'd attended.

Donnelley shook his head. "Seems to ring a dim bell. But not with the Brethren. Something else..." He thought for a moment, then laughed. "Oh, yeah. He used to be a TV evangelist in the Pacific Northwest. Oregon, Washington, northern California. Got caught with his pants down around the wrong guy's son. That was about...four, five years ago, I guess. So now he's into this, huh?"

I told him briefly about the speech I'd heard.

"Typical rhetoric. I'll let the people in the Bureau who watch these types know he's playing the game."

"So now what?" I asked. "What about Rebecca?"

"Have they contacted you a second time?"

"No."

"Well, they will. When they do, tell them you've found the money..."

"But I haven't," I said. "I don't want to play games with Rebecca's life."

Donnelley nodded his head. "I understand that, Deputy Kovak. I really do. But do you have any idea where the money is, or whatever it is, because I take it you're not sure it is money?''

"No, not really.''

"Well, do you have any idea where 'it' is?''

I shook my head. "So all we can do,'' Donnelley said, "is make them think you have 'it.' You got a positive reaction from Renfroe when you said money, right?''

Emmett and I both nodded. "Then we'll assume that's what it is. When they contact you again, and they will, you'll say you have it and make drop off plans. But remember, however they contact you, you don't do anything without speaking with the child.''

I nodded my head, too tired and too numb to do much talking.

"Deputy Kovak,'' Donnelley said, "where did you receive the first ransom note?''

I told him.

"Then I think it's a good idea if you go back to the hotel and wait there. That's where the second one will come.''

I nodded, got up, and left, driving first to the hospital to let Melissa know what was going on.

"Mama was a white supremacist?'' she said, her eyes wide.

I shook my head and smiled. "No, honey. I doubt that. Besides, the group doesn't have women in the membership. I think she found that money and took it. Pure and simple.''

Melissa started to say something, then stopped, laughing bitterly. ''I was about to ask why. What a dumb question that would have been. The poor woman had never seen more than a paycheck's worth of money in her life. I guess she just couldn't help herself. Though I'd like to think, if she'd known what it would start, she wouldn't have done it.''

''No, honey, she wouldn't have.'' I pressed her hand with mine. ''When they gonna let you outa here?''

''They're processing me now. If you can wait, you can save me calling Jewel back. She's gone to pick up the kids.''

''No problem. You got any clothes? You showed up here in a nightdress.''

She pointed to the closet. ''Jewel brought me some earlier. In there.''

I got the clothes and laid them on the bed. ''I'll go outside while you get dressed,'' I said and left.

Once in the hall, I realized it was only a short flight up and a short walk over to where Jean McDonnell's office was. I figured it was the polite thing to do. Keep her abreast of the current situation, so to speak.

I took the elevator up to her floor and walked down the hall to where the guard blocked the entrance to the locked psychiatric wing. "Deputy Kovak to see Dr. McDonnell," I said.

"Just a minute, let me call her," he said, turning to a phone on a little stand to his left. He had a name tag on. It said Curtis Allen. If I hadn't been so damn tired, the connection might have hit me sooner.

FOURTEEN

BETTE RAINTREE'S FACE wore a look of concern when I stopped at her desk outside Jean's office. Jean. Like that song back in the sixties, "Jean, Jean..." whatever. Anyway, she said, "How's Melissa doing, Mr. Kovak?"

"Healthwise okay."

"Any word on the little girl?"

I shook my head. I didn't really want to talk about it.

"Dr. McDonnell's with a patient right now." She turned and looked at the clock on the wall behind her desk. Smiling, she said, "She should be out in about five minutes though, if you'd like to wait."

There were two chairs lined up against a fake wall near the secretarial desk, so I sat down on one of them and waited. Trying to think of anything but what Rebecca was doing right that minute. In a couple of minutes, one of the orderlies came up and leaned against Bette Raintree's desk, and the two chatted. I was too tired to even listen. After a while, the door to the doctor's office opened, and Jean escorted a lady in pajamas out. The orderly took her by the arm, which the lady obviously didn't like, and led her away.

Seeing me, Jean smiled. "Well, Mr. Kovak. I've got a few minutes. Won't you come in?"

We went into her office and shut the door. Taking my hand she led me to the couch, resting her crutches against the arm, and put her arms around my neck.

"How are you holding up?" she asked.

"Not great," I said, stroking her hair with my hand. "I thought it might help to see you."

"Does it?"

"Yep."

She laughed. "Good. Because you just made my day a lot brighter, too."

I touched my lips to hers and forgot about everything for a minute or two. Then, resting our foreheads against each other, Jean said, "How's Melissa?"

"Getting dressed now. They're discharging her. I'm supposed to be taking her back home...to the hotel."

She lifted her head from mine and touched her hand to my cheek, stroking my face. I kissed her hand, then pulled it down, holding it. "Something's wrong here," I said.

"What?"

"How can you make me feel so good when I feel so goddamn bad?"

She lifted my hand to her lips, then said, "You want a clinical answer, or you want me to shut up?"

"I want you to shut up."

I was doing a dandy job of searching for her tonsils with my tongue when her intercom came on, announcing her next patient.

"How mussed up am I?" she asked, finger combing her hair.

I grinned. "You look like you just been had, lady."

I got up off the couch and moved away as she swatted me with one of her crutches. As I got to the door, she said, "If you have time tonight, come by. I'll be home."

"I don't know what will happen tonight."

"I know. I just want you to know I'm there if you need me."

"What if I just want you?"

"I'm there then, too."

I nodded and left.

I herded Melissa into the car and back to the hotel. Two of Emmett's officers were sitting in the lobby, along with what looked like some lesser fibbie types. Jasmine was at the long counter, talking discouragingly with her woeful younger sister.

Seeing me, she broke away and came up to where Melissa and I were waiting for the elevator.

"Thought I'd come by now since school should be letting out. Thought you might need me for the kids again."

"Thanks, Jasmine. But Jewel and Melissa will be here with them. I appreciate your help though. I really do."

"My pleasure," she said. Then, clearing her throat, she said to Melissa. "Milt's gonna find your girl, ma'am. He's the best."

Melissa smiled, and I shuffled my foot. "I know he will, Jasmine." The two women smiled at each other. Jasmine touched Melissa lightly on the arm and left.

I spied Harmon waiting in the lobby. Seeing me, he came forward. He kissed Melissa shyly on the cheek. "I'm so sorry, Melissa, but Milt'll find her . . . I know he will."

I just loved the way everybody thought a suspended sheriff's deputy was gonna save the day. I work so well under pressure.

"Thanks, Harmon," Melissa said, giving him the best smile she could under the circumstances.

"Milt," Harmon said, "can I talk with you a minute?"

I left Melissa standing where she was so I could keep an eye on her and moved off with Harmon. "Yeah, Harmon, what is it?"

"What we were talking about last night. . . ."

"Jesus, man, this isn't the time. . . ."

"No. Now, wait. Now's the time more than ever. It ain't safe, Milt. Not for Jewel and the kids or Melissa. Let me take 'em all to my place. . . ."

I shook my head. "They're safer here now than anywhere. We got town cops, sheriff's deputies, and FBI all over the goddamn place." I patted Harmon on the shoulder. "I understand your concern, but I think it's best if everybody stays put for a while."

Harmon nodded his head, looked around the lobby for a minute than back at me. "That little girl okay, you think, Milt?"

"I wish to hell I knew."

I went up to my room to change and ordered room service for everybody. Nobody was leaving their rooms tonight. Melissa was camping with Jewel and Marlene, and I was camping with the boys in the room next door. They were connecting rooms, so we left the door open. We all ate in Jewel's room, Harmon joining us, then the boys and Marlene moved to the other room to watch TV while us adults sat around with our thumbs up our asses and waited.

At nine o'clock the phone rang. I went to it, picking up the receiver. "Hello?"

"Milt?" It was a whisper, but a familiar one.

"Yeah?"

"It's Jean! Milt, I found her!"

"Where are you?"

"At the hosp..."

The line went dead in my hand. I stood there staring at the phone for a full second before reaction set in. I turned to Harmon. "Call Emmett. Tell him to meet me at the locked ward of the hospital. Tell him to get somebody with a gun up here with y'all."

I turned and headed for the door. Melissa caught me. "Milt!"

"I don't know, honey. Just wait."

I ran down the hall, trying not to hear Melissa's cries of anguish.

I had the gun Emmett had issued me in my holster, which I'd grabbed as I ran out the door. I laid it on the seat of the car, taking the gun out of the holster for easy access. It was as I started the car that I made the connection. The guard at the locked unit at the hospital. The name tag. Curtis Allen. One of the names Lester Bodine had given me. One of the names of known members of The Patriots for a Free America. I hadn't made the connection sooner. And because of that, not only was Rebecca in danger, but Jean was, too.

I broke every traffic law known to man, making the five miles to the hospital in just under three minutes. All told though, it had been probably five or six minutes since Jean's call. It only took a split second to kill somebody. Two split seconds to kill two somebodies.

I abandoned the '55 in front of the main entrance to the hospital, stuck the gun in back under my belt, covering it with the OU sweatshirt, and ran into the hospital and into the first available elevator. I took it to the fourth floor, then hightailed it down the hall to the entrance of the locked wing.

An Indian I knew by the name of Jimmy Littlefeather stood guard at the locked door.

"Where's Dr. McDonnell?" I asked.

"Still working, Milt. How you doing?"

"I gotta see her."

"Gotta call her. Hold on a sec..."

I grabbed Jimmy by the collar and pushed him against the wall. "I haven't got a second. Either does Dr. McDonnell. Open the goddamn door now."

"Man, I got regulations..."

I grabbed the keys off his belt and began sticking them in the key hole. On the third wrong one (in a set of something like twenty-five keys), I pulled my gun and shoved it in Jimmy's gut. "Open the goddamn door."

He did, then locked it securely behind me, no doubt calling for reinforcements. The hall was long and dimly lit. It was after nine, and all the room doors were closed, some with the muted sounds of TV shows coming through. But mostly all I heard was the sound of my footsteps going down the long hall.

I stopped at Bette Raintree's desk, in front of Jean's office door. No one was around. I went to the door and opened it, bracing myself against the wall as I did so. But the room was empty. The telephone sat on top of the desk, neat and orderly, in no way showing it had just played its own dramatic part in my ordeal.

I walked up and down the long hall of twenty rooms, ten to each side, looking in each room. In some the residents would look up at me, in most they just sat in chairs or lay on beds, staring at TVs or into their own hells.

At the end of the hall was a door marked "stairway." I pushed the door open slowly, my gun in my hand. Seeing nothing, I cautiously stepped through, hearing the door swing shut behind me with a click of finality. I looked at where I was, studying the layout. I could go up or I could go down. I went up. My feet felt like lead as I ascended the stairs, the gun pointed in front of me, my body pressed against the inside wall of the stairwell. I hit the landing and turned to go up the next flight.

At the top of that flight was Rebecca. Just like in my dream. Only she was clad in her night-clothes of the night before, her mouth taped shut, her eyes closed as if she'd been drugged. But she wasn't standing, she was slung on the hip of the orderly I'd seen earlier that day outside Jean's office. Slung on his hip like a sack of potatoes, one huge arm holding her steady. The other arm was around Jean's back, the hand with the knife in it pressed against her throat.

"Put down the gun, Deputy," the orderly said. "Put it down and kick it down the stairs."

I didn't think. If I had, maybe we'd all be dead. I just lifted the gun and fired, taking away half the man's face.

FIFTEEN

JEAN CAUGHT Rebecca as she fell out of the orderly's arm lock, falling herself since she didn't have her crutches to support her. Holstering my gun, I ran up the last flight of stairs and kicked at the prone body of the orderly. He didn't move. I bent down, putting the barrel of the gun against his temple, then feeling for a pulse, and found that shooting him again would be a bit of an overkill. He was already dead.

Jean pulled the tape off Rebecca's mouth and layed her prone on the floor, lifted the baby's head back, and reached inside her mouth. Then pressed her mouth against the child's.

"What's wrong?" I whispered, moving over quickly and kneeling near the two.

Taking a breath and bearing down gently on Rebecca's rib cage, Jean said, "One, two, she's not breathing, four..."

Again to her mouth. I'd taken CPR, but I'll be damned if I could remember one thing about it at that moment. I watched it all as if in slow motion, as Jean tried to breathe life into the little body, then pump on the little chest. It felt like hours, but in

reality it couldn't have been more than seconds before Rebecca coughed and groaned. Her big brown
eyes opened, and she looked from Jean to me.
Seeing me, she burst into tears and cried out,
"Grandpa!"

I took her into my arms and held her, with no
intention of ever letting her go. But Jean's insis-
tent tugging on my arm finally got my attention.

Whispering, Jean said, "There's another one."
She pointed upwards. "We were headed up there
to him. The day guard."

"Curtis Allen."

Jean looked at me, cocking one eyebrow.
"That's right. Anyway, he's going to come looking for us."

"How do we get out of here?"

"Shit! How the hell should I know? I've only
worked in this building less than a week!"

I whispered, "The door back into the locked
unit. It sounded like it locked...."

Jean nodded. "They all do. There's no access
into any of the floors once you're in the stairwell
without a key. Mine's on my desk."

"Then we go down."

Again she nodded, and, holding onto the stair
railing, pulled herself into a standing position.

I had my arms full with Rebecca, who felt as if
she'd fallen asleep on my shoulder. "Is she okay?"

I asked, turning my body so Jean could see the child.

She lifted one eyelid. "They doped her with something. We've got to get her out of here, Milt...."

"Can you make it?"

Jean nodded. "As long as there's a railing to hold onto."

We started down the stairs, going slowly, so slowly I wanted to scream, past the locked door to the locked ward, down, down.

"Have you ever killed anyone before?" Jean whispered.

"No," I whispered back.

"How do you feel?"

"Like being psychoanalyzed tomorrow, not at the moment, okay?"

"Freeze."

It was said with such utter boredom I almost didn't notice it. "Freeze."

I turned giving Rebecca to Jean and putting them both behind me. Curtis Allen stood three steps up, looking down at us, a slight smile on his face and an Uzi in his hand.

"Don't try nothing, Pop," he said. "One little burp and this baby'll take out all three of ya. It's a gas, man, it really, truly is. You wanna see?"

"No, thanks," I said, sounding almost as bored as he had earlier. But he wasn't bored now. Not now, not talking about his burping baby.

"You're going the right direction there, Pop," Allen said. "First, hand me your gun, real careful like...." I handed him my .45, butt first. "Now, jest keep on going down." He jerked the Uzi up and down, I supposed punctuating his remark.

I took Rebecca back from Jean and pushed Jean forward, holding onto her and the baby as best I could. Curtis Allen brought up the rear, sticking the barrel of the Uzi in my back whenever we slowed, which was often with Jean leading the way.

It seemed to take forever before we hit the basement, where Allen obviously wanted to go. He moved around us on the landing and opened the door to the basement corridor with a key. Sticking his head out the doorway, he looked both ways, obviously found all quiet, and motioned us through the door.

"This way," he said, pointing to the left. We moved forward again, Jean leading the way. Halfway down the corridor, in front of a door marked "Lab," Allen said, "Okay, stop. Now open that door."

Jean did, and we all stepped inside, Allen switching on the lights. Two rows of fluorescents lit up the room, displaying what looked like a high school chemistry lab, except bigger and meaner looking. He pointed the Uzi towards a small office off to one side, and he moved towards that. Rebecca was asleep in my arms, something I wasn't too crazy about. How could she sleep through this? What had they given her?

"Give me the kid!" Allen said, grabbing Rebecca from my arms. I struggled with him, until he pointed the Uzi at her curly dark hair, then I let her go. What else could I do?

"Now," he said, holding Rebecca on one hip. "You two, sit down in them chairs."

There were two chairs in the office, one a rolling office chair, the other a straight-legged visitor's chair. We sat, Jean in the straight-legged chair, me in the rolling one. "Okay," Allen said, looking around, seeming a little preoccupied, a little unsure of himself. "Okay, I got the kid here, right?"

I nodded my head, unable to answer him.

"Okay, so you sit. Jest sit."

Neither Jean nor I moved. Still holding onto Rebecca, he moved around the office and then the lab, looking in vain for something. Finally, out of sight, I heard him say, "Ah ha!" and he came back in with some electrical cord, but no Rebecca.

"Where's Rebecca?" I demanded.

"Huh? Oh, the kid." He pointed with his shoulder towards the lab. "I laid her on one of them tabletops in there."

I started to rise from my chair, even though he was busy trying to tie my legs. "Goddamn it! She'll fall off!"

He shoved me back down with the hand that held the Uzi. "Sit your ass down! Don't you move!"

He went back into the lab and came back with Rebecca. "Here," he said to Jean, "you hold her."

Rebecca whimpered and I panicked, jumping up again only to get hit on the head for my troubles with the butt of the Uzi. It didn't knock me out. Not totally, anyway. I fell back on my rolling chair, which began rolling towards the door to the office.

Vaguely, I heard Allen shout "goddamn it!" then felt him grab the back of the chair and pull me back into the room. It was sorta pleasant, rolling around like that. Like a merry-go-round, or a kiddie roller coaster. Through all this I could hear Jean saying, "If you hurt him, I'll castrate you! And I know how! I'm a doctor!"

Slowly, the fog was lifting, as I heard Allen say, "If there's one thing I hate worse than a pushy broad it's a gimpy pushy broad! So shut the fuck up!"

I tried to get up again, in a vain attempt to protect my woman's honor, but forgot that my legs were tied. I landed face down on the floor, saved from a broken nose in the nick of time by remembering that my arms weren't tied.

Allen sighed heavily. "Jesus H. Christ on a bicycle!" I felt him jerk me up and sit me back down on my chair. "Stay put, goddamn it!"

I felt the cord going around my shoulders and chest. "Don't talk like that," I managed to croak.

"Oh, gee whiz, I'm really sorry," Curtis Allen said. "Did I hurt your girlfriend's feelings?"

I laughed. "You know," I managed to get out, "I don't see how you guys pulled any of this off. You're all dumb as posts."

He hit me in the face, probably with the Uzi again, and I could taste blood inside my mouth. "Dumb but violent," I said.

"Milt," I heard from Jean.

"Yeah, honey?"

"Shut up."

"Okay."

Allen laughed. "That's right, lady. You tell him. Shut the fuck up, Milty baby."

Still laughing, he left the office. I could see him in the lab, passing through on his way to the door, which I could hear him lock behind him.

"You okay?" I asked Jean.

"Yes. You?"

"As well as can be expected. How's Rebecca?"

"Not good. They've drugged her, Milt."

"Shit."

I began pushing against the cord around my chest. "Stop!" Jean said. "You're making it tighter on Rebecca and me!"

I relaxed. "Sorry," I said. "You mean he's got the two of you tied together?"

"Yes, she's on my lap. You pull too hard on your end, you could choke her."

"How are your hands?"

There was a short silence, then Jean replied, "Just fine, thank you. Why in the hell do you ask?"

"Are they loose?"

"Yes."

"Can you work them so you can slide Rebecca out, like between your legs to the floor? If you can, there'll be enough slack where we can get this shit off."

"Okay, I'll try." I could feel the cord tighten against me, loosen, tighten, loosen, tighten.

"How's it going?"

"Shhh!"

I could feel her wriggling in her chair, then felt the slackness as Rebecca was eased out of the cord and onto the floor.

I hurriedly pulled the cord off my shoulders and Jean's and then bent down to untie my legs. By the time I got over to Jean, Rebecca was back in her lap. I untied Jean's legs, which was a bitch to do since Allen had very creatively threaded the cord through her braces and the chair legs.

"We've got to get Rebecca upstairs, Milt," Jean said. "I don't like the way she's breathing."

I grabbed the baby out of her arms and helped Jean up. Slowly, we progressed to the door of the lab. Which was locked solid. "Goddamn it shit," I said.

Jean looked at me. "Goddamn it shit?"

I looked at her. "That doesn't make any sense," she said.

"Since when are swear words supposed to make sense?"

"Well, there should be some symmetry. Alliteration if nothing else."

"Goddamn fuck shit. Is that more symmetrical?" I asked, turning and twisting the doorknob for the hundred-eleventh time.

"No, not really."

"I'll work on it."

I kicked the door. The metal made an interesting sound but didn't budge.

"Any suggestions?" I asked, looking over my shoulder at Jean.

"Yes. Give me Rebecca. You can't bust through that door holding onto her."

"I've got news for you, lady. I can't bust through that door unless maybe I'm holding a jackhammer or a blowtorch! This thing's metal, and it ain't budging."

"Do you have a credit card?" she asked.

I sighed. "You can't card a door like this."

"How do you know unless you try?"

"Because I'm a peace officer and I know these things. Trust me."

She took Rebecca from my arms. "Appease me. Just try."

"Shit." I took my wallet out of my back pocket and got my Sears card out. The only one I own. I slipped it in the space between the two doors, wiggled it around the locking mechanism, and heard a distinct click. I turned the knob and opened the door.

"Don't say it," I said to Jean.

She smiled sweetly, every dimple going a mile an hour. "Say what?"

I closed the door quietly with us still on the inside. "What are you doing?" Jean asked.

"I ain't going out there unarmed."

"Well, that's okay, lab techs always keep an arsenal lying around. God, Milt!"

"Just a minute! Just a minute!"

I wandered around the lab, looking for something, anything to help protect us. Finally, I noticed the filing cabinets. They were the kind with metal davits attached to each cabinet with a heavy metal bar running through that's padlocked at the top. Except none of them were padlocked. I pulled out two bars, took Rebecca back in my arms, and handed one bar to Jean. "Can you use this like a crutch? Unless you have to use it like a billy club?"

She nodded her head and we went back to the door. I opened it slowly, peeking around the corner. The corridor was empty. We moved out, Jean behind me, leaning heavily on the metal bar, me in the lead, holding onto the dead weight that was Rebecca in my arms, my metal bar at the ready for whoever we might meet.

We'd only gone a few steps when I saw the opened door, and the light spilling into the corridor. I motioned Jean against the wall and handed Rebecca to her, then crept to the open doorway. On the other side of which was Curtis Allen, deep in a one-sided conversation, obviously a phone call he hadn't wanted us to hear.

"Well, whatja want me to do with 'em? . . . Then what? Jest dump the bodies? Shit, man! . . . No, I ain't squeamish! Shit! I done this before, ya know. . . . But he's a cop. . . . Okay, okay."

I heard the phone slam down. Heard footsteps coming toward the door. I lifted my metal rod. When Curtis Allen came through the doorway, I pretended his head was meant for a line drive to take me all the way home.

Curtis Allen lay on the floor, flat on his back, blood running out of his broken nose and one tooth dangling out of his mouth. I reached down and pulled the tooth the rest of the way out, least he swallow the damn thing and choke to death. Didn't want that.

Jean called from her place leaning against the corridor wall. "You get him?"

"Yeah."

"Is he dead?"

"No, but he's gonna have a hell of a headache."

Just then I heard footsteps coming down the stairway, the door to which was directly across from where Jean and Rebecca stood. I moved quickly in front of them, holding my metal rod up like Mickey Mantle in his finest hour. The door opened slowly. I adjusted my grip. Flexed my fingers. A hand appeared at the open door, a gun in the hand. I raised the metal rod and brought it down hard as I could on the hand. The gun flew out, someone yelled in pain, and I went for the gun, spread-eagle on the floor, twisted, turned and held the gun on the man in the doorway. My old buddy, Emmett.

"Goddamn, Milt, I think you done broke it," he said, holding his limp wrist with the good hand he had left.

I got myself up off the floor and went over to him. "Hey, man, I'm sorry...."

"Sorry? Sorry! Jesus Christ, you done broke my hand!"

"Milt!" Jean said. "Rebecca ... we have to get her upstairs!"

Emmett stopped looking at his wrist for a moment. "You found her?"

"Yeah, and the guys that got her." I pointed to Curtis Allen laying in the doorway.

"That one upstairs yours too?" Emmett asked. I nodded my head. "Shit, I guess I'm lucky my hand's all you did," he said, but he was grinning.

"We gotta get Rebecca upstairs," I said, turning and taking the drugged child out of Jean's arms. "She's been drugged."

"Then let's use the elevator, okay? Take this here key," Emmett said, shoving his hip pocket at me.

We made it to the second floor pediatric nurses' station where Jean started hollering for a gurney and this med and that med, taking it all away from me and Emmett, who just stood there watching it all.

Jean turned to me. "I'm going to pump her stomach. God only knows how much shit they gave her. It's better to be safe than sorry."

I nodded as she hurried off, being helped by a nurse as she yelled to one of the orderlies to get up to the fourth floor and get her goddamn crutches. And be quick about it. God, I love a forceful woman.

Emmett sent his men down to get Curtis Allen, and then we had a nurse look at his hand. "Looks broken to me," she said.

"Lucile, you think maybe you got a doctor 'round here might wanna look at this? Take an X ray? Something like that?" Emmett asked.

Lucile smiled. "Sure, Chief. Whatever makes you happy."

I walked up to the nurses' station and asked for a phone, then dialed the Longbranch. After a minute I had Melissa on the line.

After a brief conversation with her, I joined Emmett and we left the hospital, heading for the police station where Curtis Allen was already being held. Once in the interrogation room, we began our questions.

For which we got no answer except, "Where's my fucking lawyer?"

SIXTEEN

"YOU WANNA HOTDOG or one of them sausages on a stick?" I ask.

"Sausage, I guess," Glenda Sue answers.

I order two sausages on sticks and two Diet Pepsis and we head back to our bleacher seats. As we walk sideways across our row over the bent knees of our neighbors, I look out on the field. They've build a makeshift Berlin Wall out there, and standing on top are a couple of high school kids with phony (I hope) M-16s and make-believe East German uniforms.

The loudspeaker whines, and then we hear the voice of Mr. Hoover, the high school football coach and MC for the finale of Pioneer Week.

"In 1962, the world was split in two by the erection of a wall of stone. The Berlin Wall—the most ominous structure known to mankind. Families were torn apart. A country. A world... But now, in 1989, after 27 long, long years..."

A bugle sounds and two hundred high school kids run onto the field and begin tearing at the wall. It crumbles before our eyes. Everybody in the bleachers stands, the cheers are deafening. I feel heat behind my eyes, a roll in my stomach. Not unlike the feeling I get every time I watch a telephone company commercial.

"Ain't this great!" I shout at Glenda Sue. She's smiling. She nods her head. Impulsively, for her, she turns and kisses me. I kiss her back.

"Let's get married," I say.

The smile leaves her face as she turns back to the scene on the football field. The shards of "Berlin Wall" are being removed, while the high school marching band parades onto the field playing "Edelweiss." Which I think is Austrian, not German, but what the hey. It's the thought that counts.

The cheering has stopped as I turn again to Glenda Sue. "Did you hear me?" I ask.

"That's stupid," she says.

"What? 'Edelweiss'?"

"No. Us getting married."

"Why?"

"I've been married. And so have you. I figure being that stupid once is enough for anybody."

"Well, you ain't LaDonna, and I sure as hell ain't Linn. Our marriage would be different."

Glenda Sue is quiet, looking at the marching band on the field.

"I swear to God, Milt, all you ever do is give me grief."

I sat up in bed and lit a cigarette. Maybe my last.
Maybe not. *"I swear to God, Milt, all you ever do
is give me grief."* That's what she'd said. Grief.
Now I guess I was the one with the grief. Oh,
Glenda Sue. Jesus. But mixed up with all that grief,
I knew, was a hell of a lot of guilt. And most of it
had to do with Jean McDonnell. How could I feel
like I did about her, about Jean, with Glenda Sue
barely in her grave? How could my palms sweat
and my knees go weak every time I saw Jean?
When they never sweated or went weak over
Glenda Sue? I pondered those questions for a
while, until it dawned on me. All these thoughts I'd
been having about Glenda Sue. They weren't about
the lover I'd had for the past couple of years. They
were about the best friend I'd had for over forty
years. Little Glenda Sue Rainey. If Glenda had
been a Glenn, there'd have been no problem when
we ran into each other again. We'd of got drunk
together, chased women together, talked about
manly things. But we were both products of the
times in which we were raised. And men and
women weren't friends. They were lovers. Glenda
Sue hadn't wanted to marry me. Maybe even she
didn't know exactly why, discounting of course her
plane ticket of the next day. But even without that,
she wouldn't have wanted to. We'd messed it all up,
becoming lovers. We talked to each other like lov-

ers, yelling and spitting one minute, in bed the next. But the kind of love we had, really had, wasn't meant for that kinda scene. We should have been crying on each other's shoulders about other women, other men. Talking about our feelings, shit like that. I went to bed that night and cried myself to sleep, like somebody who'd just lost their best friend.

The next morning I met Michael Donnelley, the fibbie in the generic suit, for breakfast at the Longbranch, filling him in on the night before. And it had been a long night. Rebecca's stomach was pumped, and she was resting comfortably at the hospital, her mother in a chair next to her bed. I had spent several hours with the county attorney explaining why I had shot the orderly. We had the kidnappers of Rebecca, but little else. One was dead, and one wasn't talking. How it all tied into Glenda Sue, I for one sure didn't know.

That is, not until Maynard Dabney walked out of his office and into the restaurant. At that point Donnelley looked up, saw the Longbranch's head honcho, and said, "Well, I'll be damned. It's Andrew J. Minike."

The next night I laid in bed with Jean, touching the smoothness of her skin with my fingertips, absolutely drunk with the knowledge that nobody else had ever done that very thing I was doing.

"I'm confused," Jean said.

I kissed her neck. "Let me enlighten you...."

She laughed. "Not about that, dummy. I'm a doctor. *That* doesn't confuse me. I mean, what did Maynard Dabney have to do with it?"

I leaned back on the pillow, staring up at her rose-colored ceiling fan. "Everything. See, Dabney's real name is Andrew J. Minike, and he used to be the top dog in this thing called the United Aryan Brethren. This group of fine young men who felt the best thing for America would be if it was all white. And all Protestant."

"Humph," Jean Marie McDonnell, product of Chicago's Catholic schools, said.

"Anyway, they thought the best way of doing this was by robbing armored cars, selling arms, knocking over liquor stores, etc., etc. Anyway, the FBI caught 'em about six years ago. All but the ringleader, Minike. About fifty of 'em went to jail, and the rest of the membership, about two hundred lovely souls, went about their everyday business, or so the FBI thought. Except Minike reorganized, got some of his old troop and moved here to Prophesy County and bought the Longbranch. With a little talking in the right dumb ears, he was able to start his nasty shit up again here, except 'Dabney' was removed from it all. He just rented them the room."

"So what does all this have to do with Glenda Sue?"

"According to records they found in a locked box in Dabney's office, he's been laundering money through the Patriots for a Free America. Remember the $10,000 contribution I told you about?" She nodded. "Well, it was really $100,000. They'd record ten percent of whatever it was they were laundering that week. Just honest donations to a 'worthwhile' cause. Shit, it was even tax deductible. Marty Vanderhoff was the only one in the Patriots from Longbranch that knew where the money was coming from. That it was coming straight from Dabney. Dabney's not talking about it, but I figure with Glenda Sue's murder and the kidnapping, Vanderhoff was getting scared. Maybe scared enough to talk. That's why he and his wife were killed.

"The best we can piece this thing together is Glenda Sue found a stash of the money to be laundered. And she took it."

"Who killed her?"

"According to Curtis Allen, it was Bo Nieson, the guy that had the knife to your throat. The orderly."

Jean shivered. "Oh, wonderful. I'm glad you blew him away."

"Let's don't get into that."

"Well, I'm not going to lie, Milt. I am glad."

"Anyway, also according to Allen, Dabney ordered the hit on Glenda Sue and the searching of her place and my place. And Rebecca's kidnapping. Curtis Allen said they all got a big kick out of taking Rebecca. Her being what she is."

"Jesus. But where's the money?" she asked.

"God only knows."

She lay there in my arms a minute, then lifted up on one elbow to look at me. "Are you okay?" I rolled my eyes and she swatted me with her hand. "I'm not asking you that from a psychiatrist's point of view. I'm asking as a friend...and lover."

"As a friend," I said, "I'm okay. As a lover, I'm fucking wonderful."

And we didn't talk about it anymore that night.

The next day I walked into the sheriff's office and put up with the hug from Gladys and the handshakes from the guys and made my way back to Elberry's office. The sheriff sat in his big swivel chair, looking out the window.

"Elberry," I said upon entering the room.

He swiveled around, smiled, stood up, and extended his hand. "Milt. It's good to have you back with us."

I didn't take his hand. Instead I sat down in one of his visitor's chairs and looked at him, hard. He sat back and stared at me. Finally, he cleared his throat. "Okay. I'm guilty of bad judgment. But that's all. I didn't know nothing about Glenda Sue or the little girl. And if you say you don't believe that, Milt, you're a fucking liar."

I nodded my head. "Oh, I believe that, Elberry. But I believe you're guilty of more than bad judgment. I know Dabney gave you a deer lease. What else you get from him? Use of his fishing boat? Maybe a cabin? Help on that new deck you built at your house? What else?"

"I thought he was a friend, Milt. That's all."

"You let that friendship influence you, Sheriff. You tried to hinder the investigation when it started getting too close to your friend. You tried to use your influence to keep everybody away from Dabney. You stripped me of my power twice to help your 'friend.'"

"Milt, you and me been friends for a long time...."

"Yes, sir, we have. And you been sheriff here a long time. Maybe too long."

He laughed. "You saying you're running against me next spring?"

I shook my head. "No, sir. I'm saying you're giving it up now. Poor health. Whatever. You turn in your badge now, and I don't go to the FBI with your involvement. Now even if I did go to them, chances are they could never force you out. But it would be all over the papers. It would go hard on Nadine and your mama.''

I could see him touch the butt of his gun on the hip holster he wore. I wondered for a minute if he would really shoot me, but he didn't. He put his hands on top of his desk. Then reached back down and pulled out the .45, handing it over to me, butt first. He took the badge off his breast pocket and laid that down on the desk.

''My last official act will be to make you acting sheriff until the next election. That okay with you?''

I nodded my head while he went out to Gladys to get the paperwork done.

SEVENTEEN

IT WAS ALL OVER the papers for about two weeks, and they played it up big. "Nest of Nazis Nipped in Longbranch," "Fascists Found and Finished." Davey Guy and his family were gone for good it seemed, and the other members, the ones from Longbranch who'd gotten caught up in it, were keeping real low profiles. The membership from Dabney/Minike's original organization was being detained by the Feds.

Two weeks after it was over, Melissa and Rebecca went with Jewel and me and the kids to church one Sunday. You'd a thought by the reception they got they were royalty. Later that day, Melissa and I talked about the future.

"You staying here or going back to 'Weird-a-fornia'?"

She sighed. "I don't know, Milt. At first, right after I got Rebecca back, I knew I'd get out of here. But now..." She laughed. "Hell, the way the town's acting, as guilty as everyone's feeling, just by association, Rebecca could be voted homecoming queen tomorrow."

"This is a good town, honey. People are just scared. Most of the livelihoods around here were made in the oil patch, even if it was indirectly. Everything's tied to that. When it all went to shit, they had to have somebody to blame it on. But I think this . . . incident maybe cleared the air. Got people back to thinking rationally. It's a good place to raise a child, Melissa. It really is."

She smiled at me. "Maybe it is. And now that I have such an extended family, you and Jewel and the kids, it would seem a shame to go back to California."

I smiled back at her, and we left it at that.

On December 19, three weeks after Rebecca had been found, Jean accompanied me to my wife's wedding. Okay, my ex-wife's wedding. Whatever. It was a lovely ceremony at the First Presbyterian of Bishop. You know what a Presbyterian is, don't you? A Methodist that makes over $50,000 a year. Leave it to Dwayne Dickey to be a Presbyterian.

The only thing out of kilter, other than being there in the first place, was the fact that the bride was wearing white. I didn't think women were supposed to do that. The second time, I mean. I was living proof that she had no right to be wearing white. Up until the vandalism, I still had the bed she'd been deflowered on. Sentimental fool that I am.

Oh, well, there's nothing for the old libido like going to your ex-wife's wedding. In a few months, I'd be attending another one. This one as best man. Old Harmon had finally gotten around to asking the front question that goes with Jewel Anne moving in with him. Namely, marriage. They were already writing their vows, which were going to include Jewel's three kids and Harmon's two. I figured they were letting themselves in for an interesting life together.

I was seeing Dr. Marston by myself now, since my problems with Jewel were over. As soon as she accepted Harmon's proposal, I told her flat out she wasn't putting pickled wood in my kitchen. Now I was going to counseling to deal with the fact that I'd killed a man. Something I'd never done before, not in the Air Force, not on duty as a sheriff's deputy. There was no doubt in my mind that that particular fella needed killing, it was just dealing with the fact that I'd done it.

I spent the night of my ex-wife's wedding at Jean's house, and the next morning I packed her luggage in the back of my '55 and we headed for Tulsa, to the airport where she'd make her flight to Chicago for Christmas with her family.

"I kinda hoped we could have Christmas together," I said, or whined, or whatever.

She patted my knee. "I know. Maybe some other time."

"Christmas comes but once a year."

"Thank you, I wasn't aware of that."

"Why are you being so snippy?" I asked.

"I'm not being snippy. I'm being . . . sarcastic."

"Oh, well, that's so much better."

"I'm glad you can appreciate the difference."

I drove in silence as she made little rat-a-tat-tat sounds with her fingernails on the dashboard of my car.

"Why are you so nervous?" I asked.

"I don't like flying."

"Then don't fly. Stay here with me."

"Very funny."

"I wasn't trying to be funny."

"That's usually when you're at your most hilarious," she said.

"Boy, isn't this a fun trip?" I said to the world in general.

Finally, we pulled into the circle in front of the Tulsa airport.

"Just let me off in front," Jean said.

"Hey, I was gonna park the car, take you in, have our farewell scene in the airport. I love those!"

"I'd rather have it right here. In the car."

I pulled into the white zone, got out of the car, and got her luggage out of the trunk. Handing it to a skycap, I stood next to the car as she maneuvered her way out, got her crutches under her arms, and turned to me.

"Milt, I'm going to be gone for close to two weeks."

I nodded my head. "I know that," I said.

"And you've got some thinking to do in those two weeks."

"Okay. About what?"

She turned and headed for the doors, taking two steps, then turning her head towards me. "About whether or not we're going to keep the baby."

She turned again and walked off, ignoring my question of, "What baby? Jean? Oh, Jean!"

Christmas Eve I lay in bed exhausted. I'd just put together a junior pool table and a ten-speed bike for Carl, a dollhouse and a Barbie Corvette for Rebecca, a stereo for Marlene, and a VCR and TV for Leonard. I was exhausted. I'd just gotten to sleep when a firm hand woke me up.

"Wha..."

"Milt!" It was a loud whisper.

I opened my eyes and saw Melissa looking down at me. "Wake up, Milt."

I leaned up on one elbow. "What is it?"

"I know where it is."

"What?"

"The money."

I looked at her for a long moment, then it finally dawned on me what she was talking about. I swung my legs out of bed and sat there for a minute, rubbing my face to wake myself up.

"What are you talking about?"

Melissa sat down on the bed next to me. "When I was little, about ten, I had a puppy. His name was Jasper...."

"That's sweet, but..."

She hit my arm to shut me up. "My father got mad because Jasper peed on his shoes one night, so he wrung his neck."

"Oh, baby," I said, slipping my arm across her shoulders.

"Yeah, no big deal. We both know he was an asshole. Anyway, the next day Mama and I buried Jasper in a shoe box out behind the trailer, under Mama's wisteria vine. Then a couple of years later, Daddy came into some money. Won it shooting craps or something. Anyway, Mama and I sat up one night when he was drunk counting the money in his pockets. And she said ... Milt, she said, 'If I thought I could get away with it, I'd take this money and hide it out where we buried Jasper. Nobody but you and me would ever know where it was hidden.''

Melissa and I looked at each for a full minute before I got up, we both got dressed, and we left the house, going to the shed for a shovel, then driving the '55 out to Glenda Sue's trailer. Taking a flashlight, Melissa led me directly to the spot where her long-ago puppy had been buried.

With Melissa holding the wisteria vine back, I put the shovel to the cold ground and used my foot to press it into the earth. One shovelful and we'd uncovered the shoe box, full of holes and earth-stained. Next to it were several Tupperware containers.

Melissa got down on her hands and knees and began opening the boxes. And all that money spilled out. We sat there on the cold ground and counted it: $980,000. Twenty thousand shy of a million.

"Jesus Christ," Melissa said. "No wonder Mama couldn't help herself."

I shook my head. "Mighty tempting."

"Yeah," Melissa said, looking at me sideways, "ain't it just?"

"Why are you looking at me like that?"

Melissa got to her knees, the better to plead and beg. "Nobody knows about this except you and me, Milt. Nobody. I don't make that much at the hospital. Not enough for Rebecca's education. You want Rebecca to have an inferior education, Milt?

You want her to have to live off other people the rest of her life? Like we're living off you now?''

"Stop it, Melissa."

I bundled the money up. The day after Christmas, I drove to Oklahoma City to the office of the Federal Bureau of Investigation and turned in $500,000. I figured half the change could buy a lot of diapers.

Take 3 books and a surprise gift FREE

SPECIAL LIMITED-TIME OFFER

Mail to: The Mystery Library™
        3010 Walden Ave.
        P.O. Box 1867
        Buffalo, N.Y. 14269-1867

YES! Please send me 3 free books from the Mystery Library™ and my free surprise gift. Then send me 3 mystery books, first time in paperback, every month. Bill me only $3.69 per book plus 25¢ delivery and applicable sales tax, if any*. There is no minimum number of books I must purchase. I can always return a shipment at your cost simply by dropping it in the mail, or cancel at any time. Even if I never buy another book from The Mystery Library™, the 3 free books and surprise gift are mine to keep forever.   415 BPY AJJU

Name   (PLEASE PRINT)

Address   Apt. No.

City   State   Zip

*Terms and prices subject to change without notice. N.Y. residents add applicable sales tax. This offer is limited to one order per household and not valid to present subscribers.
© 1990 Worldwide Library.   MYS-93R

A FLOWER IN THE DESERT

First Time in Paperback

A JOSHUA CROFT MYSTERY

Walter Satterthwait

Santa Fe private investigator Joshua Croft doesn't like his new case...or Roy Alonzo. The actor's messy divorce had made headlines when his ex-wife, Melissa, accused him of molesting their daughter. Now, mother and child have disappeared, and Melissa's sister is found tortured to death.

Following a trail from Beverly Hills to a remote New Mexico commune, Croft confronts the endless veils of secrecy behind which Melissa appeared to live, move and hide. It's dangerously clear Melissa is a wanted woman—dead or alive!

"Satterthwait writes a charging-ahead mystery...."
—*Minneapolis Star-Tribune*

Available in December at your favorite retail stores.
Also available are two earlier titles by this popular author.

#83265 WALL OF GLASS
#83266 AT EASE WITH THE DEAD

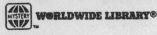

COFFIN AND THE PAPER MAN

Gwendoline Butler

First Time in Paperback

A
JOHN
COFFIN
MYSTERY

A PROMISE OF DELIVERY

Sixteen-year-old Anna Mary Kinver is raped and stabbed in the dank Rope Alley section of Leathergate. A former psychiatric patient, covered with blood, is picked up for questioning and subsequently let go.

Soon thereafter, John Coffin, chief commander of the Docklands district, receives the first in a series of notes from an anonymous letter writer calling himself "the Paper Man," who promises more bodies if Anna Mary's killer is not caught.

As the case goes unsolved, more bodies turn up. Who is the Paper Man?

"Coffin...solves a complex puzzle in this richly textured police procedural."
—*Kirkus Reviews*

Available in December at your favorite retail stores.